SEASON OF THE WITCH

Books by Melissa Bobe

SEASON OF THE WITCH
ELECTRIC TREES
NASCENT WITCH
SIBYLS

SEASON OF THE WITCH

A NOVELLA BY MELISSA BOBE

The Hive Press ● New York

This is a work of fiction. All names, characters, organizations, events, and places are either products of the author's imagination or are used fictitiously. Any resemblance to actual places, events, or persons, living or dead, is purely coincidental.

SEASON OF THE WITCH

Copyright © 2023 Melissa Bobe
All rights reserved.

ISBN-13: 9798399813998

A Hive Press Book

Cover art & design by Melissa Bobe

This book is typeset in GT Alpina.

For all you library witches out there—
the ones I've worked alongside, and
the ones I'll never meet.
Never doubt that the world needs you,
especially now.

Y para mis abuelitas—
I hope I'm making you both very proud.

ONE

The moon was an echo of what it had been at its fullest point every night that year, seeming almost translucent in the sky above the woods that bordered the small town of Mire. But there was something about its thinness, its veil-like fragility, that spoke of a change in the world beneath it. This great mirror in the sky that reflected light onto those below now took on the hue of their own hesitancies and doubts, and something more, something tremulous and filled with potential...

Endicott Thyne was sure that she had seen a moon like this once before. She glanced at the clock on the wall as a shiver told her to tear her eyes from the sky she'd been gazing at through the window. And with concern and with purpose, she caught the stroke of midnight that never sounded, for the hour arrived but the clock was silent, and so was the room, the house, and the world beyond.

Endicott went to the bookshelf and sought out a volume that in the ten years since she'd taken ownership of her grandmother's home, she'd never had reason to open. She found what she was looking for, marked by a lock of her own baby hair tied about a small photograph of her that said on the back in her grandmother's unmistakable calligraphy, "E's first birthday – Full Moon, Season of the Witch."

And it had taken thirty years to arrive again, but Endicott knew that time was as likely to repeat itself as anything else. What it might mean, her grandmother was not around to tell her, so Endicott did what any sensible witch would do: she dug into the back pocket of her jeans, pulled out her cell phone, and called her best friend.

"Are you seeing this? Well, what do you think... No, I have enough gas. All right, I'll be there." She got ready to hang up, then quickly added, "Wait, wait—do you have any chocolate? Because I need the caffeine and I'm not drinking coffee in the middle of the night. No, chocolate's not going to give me the same stomach problems. Whatever—fine. See you soon."

Endicott grabbed a bag, threw in a few crystals and an herb satchel for good measure, then slipped into her driving loafers. She put the baby picture of herself in the pocket of her jeans not occupied by her phone, snatched her car keys from the table where she'd thrown them, and headed out her front door into the strange but familiar night.

*   *   *

When she arrived at the bridge, Gabriela was waiting for her in a floor-length, neon-yellow dress that she must have made herself, because Endicott doubted there was a store in existence that would stock it, never mind one in Mire. Gabriela waved at her like an air traffic controller, and as Endicott slowed to a stop, she saw the glint of wrappers on bars of chocolate, one in each of her friend's hands.

"Ridiculous," she murmured, but a grin split her face nevertheless.

As she stepped out to meet Gabriela, she caught sight of two other silhouettes at the edge of the bridge.

"You had time to find me chocolate and gather company," she greeted Gabriela. "I'm impressed."

"We thought it prudent to come along," a voice in the darkness said before Gabriela could speak. "It's not like any of us could have missed that moon."

"And yet there are only two of you," Endicott replied dryly. "Is it not as bright on the other side?"

"Mind your manners, Enny," Gabriela chided her gently. "It's not like we're a coalition in and of ourselves."

The two witches that had been in darkness stepped forward. The one who'd addressed Endicott wore a pair of tailored grey slacks topped by a cream sleeveless blouse, and a silvery watch glinted against the deep brown skin of her wrist as she crossed her arms. Her black hair was styled in an elegant high bun, showing off the long nape of her neck.

The other witch was wearing a lacey pink high-collar dress and brown leather boots that went up to her mid-thighs. Her long brown curls, not dissimilar in color and shine to Gabriela's own thick waves, trailed down her back, and she had a large pink rose pinned behind one ear. She said in a light and echoing voice, "You'll have to forgive Xandra. She tends to get a little dramatic when the moon does strange things."

"I wonder what that's like," Endicott replied, glancing up and down Gabriela's dress pointedly.

"I was going to wear this tonight regardless," her best friend told her, hand on one neon hip.

"So, are we going to discuss this?" Xandra asked impatiently. "Or did Maritza and I drag ourselves out of bed and down into Mire for nothing?"

A goose suddenly called out in the night, loud and agitated.

"Whose is that?" Endicott wanted to know.

Maritza blushed. "She's not usually so vocal."

"You keep geese?" Gabriela's tone wasn't as judgmental as Endicott's had been, but she was clearly intrigued. Gabriela herself kept a small drove of hares, and bees, of course, as all witches did, but as far as Endicott knew, not a witch in Mire had ever kept geese.

"Just the one. She was a foundling," Maritza explained. "I wasn't about to leave her orphaned and alone."

"Of course," Gabriela murmured, and Endicott recognized the kind smile that almost always lit her best friend's face upon meeting someone new. Gabriela loved making friends almost as much as she did making dresses. "Well, I brought enough chocolate for all of us. Should we set up camp out here?"

They shared a collective shrug. "May as well," Xandra said, relaxing a little for the first time. "We should probably keep an eye on the bridge, after all, even if just for the rest of the night."

The bridge connected Mire to the town of Ember Hollow, which was larger several times over and where witches were more populous but also more dispersed. As far back as she could remember, Endicott had known the bridge was of great significance to the witches of both towns, but like most of her peers, she didn't exactly know why. Theoretically, a crossroads of any sort could be used to tap into great power, but that didn't necessarily explain why this one bridge should be so important.

They settled down on the soft earth, and Xandra and Maritza used their magic to light a small fire around which they sat as Gabriela, priorities always in mind, murmured a gentle chant to keep the grass from staining their clothes. Though there was a long history of tension between the Mire witches and those that lived in Ember Hollow, Endicott felt at ease in such a circle, her powers at rest alongside others just like her. It was probably what non-witches felt at Thanksgiving: you might not like all of your cousins, but there was comfort in gathering.

"Does anyone ever feel like we're wandering around without a roadmap that someone who came before should've left for us?" Gabriela said, as though reading her best friend's thoughts. "I mean, I know that moon is important, but I'll be damned if I have any idea why."

Maritza's goose had settled itself against her leg, curled up like any creature a witch might keep. For her part, Endicott was quietly pleased she wasn't the only one present who kept a solitary animal, though there was no way her hawk would've come with her to this meeting. Unlike Maritza's goose, he would not leave his nest in the middle of the night just to keep tabs on his witch, exceptional moon or not. She knew it was likely that Gabriela's hares were hopping around somewhere not far off, but they, too, were independent by nature and wouldn't show up unless needed.

Xandra frowned. "Ember Hollow keeps pretty good historical records, at least as our kind go. But I understand what you're saying—it's hard not to dwell on the fact that we've got more questions than answers with that moon up above."

"I have a small clue." Endicott fished in her back pocket to retrieve the photograph of herself. She handed it to Gabriela, whose eyebrows raised in surprise as the witches passed the image around their small circle.

"Season of the Witch? That...rings a bell, of a sort," Maritza said finally.

"I agree," murmured Xandra. "I've heard it—or read it—before. But I can't recall where, when, why..."

"So we're still stumbling around in the dark," Gabriela sighed.

"Not necessarily," Maritza said, making eye contact with Xandra.

"Salomé?"

"I don't know who else."

"Who's Salomé?" Endicott interjected, not liking the feeling that there was even more she was missing beyond the mysterious moon.

"Library witch," Xandra explained. "The best Ember Hollow has to offer."

"I wish we still had a witch in our library," Gabriela said, then shot Endicott a gentle glance. Mire's last librarian had been Endicott's grandmother.

"Salomé's fun," Maritza told them with a smile. "You'll like her."

"A fun librarian?" Endicott asked skeptically. Her grandmother had been many things—powerful, thoughtful, brilliant—but "fun" wouldn't exactly fall high on Endicott's list of descriptors of the woman.

"She keeps salamanders. You know, because of her name?" Maritza shrugged. "She's into wordplay. I guess it's a library witch thing."

"Do you remember the moon from that year?" Xandra asked Endicott, still holding the baby photograph. "I mean, I know you were little, but you'll recall more than we can. Maritza and I weren't even born until a year or so later."

Gabriela leaned forward with interest, studying her friend. "That's right, Enny—you're a year older than me, too. Can you remember anything from that far back?"

Endicott nodded. "I've seen a moon like this before."

They were all silent for a moment, but if the others were waiting for Endicott to elaborate, she couldn't help but disappoint. The most she knew was that once she'd glimpsed a similar moon. Memory didn't serve her beyond that.

"So, when can you two come out to Ember Hollow?" Maritza wanted to know. "I'm sure Salomé will be glad to speak with all of us."

"Tomorrow works for me," Gabriela said. "Endicott?"

But Endicott's attention had been drawn back to the bridge. She took off her glasses and cleaned them on her shirt to be sure, but she wasn't imagining things. There was something about the bridge as it stood under the moon, something that made it look like it was moving or breathing, or...

Xandra followed her gaze and stood, trying to get a better look against the contrast of the fire they'd made and the dark of the night around them. "Are those...?"

The witches were all on their feet now, moving as a group towards the bridge. Maritza's goose refused to accompany her, hanging nervously back by the fire.

"That's not like her at all," Maritza remarked, frowning, but she continued forward with her peers.

A closer look revealed dozens upon dozens of rats, coating the surface of the bridge. They seemed to be coming from its center, and they were running in the only two directions available to them: towards Mire, and towards Ember Hollow.

"Well, that's...different," Gabriela said.

A mischief wasn't a bad thing, per se. Witches had been known to occasionally keep rats, though they weren't a common choice of creature in modern times. But these rats moved in such a frenzy and such great numbers that Endicott had to wonder whether they belonged to a witch at all. And she realized, after a moment, there was something else strange about them.

"They're not squeaking," she told the others. "They're not making any sound at all."

Xandra nodded, frowning. "When a creature is silent, it's usually waiting on its witch to...well, do *something*."

"We'll come your way tomorrow," Endicott said. "I think the sooner we meet your library witch, the better."

TWO

Salomé was nothing like Endicott's grandmother, which she had expected. There weren't many people like Dorothea Thyne in Mire or Ember Hollow, as far as she knew. But what she didn't expect was a woman whose wardrobe rivaled Gabriela's in brightness and color.

"Oh, I like this witch already," Gabriela murmured to Endicott, grinning as they followed Xandra and Maritza through the front reading room of the Ember Hollow library, towards the reference desk where Salomé sat draped in gauzy fabrics of fuchsia and tangerine, lilac glasses balanced on the end of her nose. "Did your grandmother know her?"

Endicott shrugged. "I honestly wouldn't have thought to ask."

Her grandmother had raised Endicott after her mother had been killed. She remembered moving from the edges of Ember Hollow over the bridge to Mire, which back then had seemed as strange to her as it did small. At ten years old, if someone had told Endicott that she would eventually come to feel her grandmother's house in Mire was more of a home than any she'd known previously, she would have laughed.

The house smelled of the things her grandmother was made of: witchcraft, honeycomb, and books. Unlike her mother's small, solitary Langstroth on the roof of their apartment building in Ember Hollow, the five majestic hives of Dorothea Thyne hummed loudly enough to lull Endicott into unwilling sleep during that first week in Mire, when she had been determined to stay awake in protest of being transplanted to a town that was not her own. But the bees seemed to insist with their droning that she was in fact theirs, and that she belonged to Mire, as well. She rested, dreamless, night after night, spared any visions of the mother she'd lost and the catastrophe that had claimed her life.

"How fascinating," a bubbling voice greeted them now. "It's not often Xandra Davis and Maritza Menendez grace our library with their presence. And you've brought along one of the Thyne witches, who have not been seen in Ember Hollow in some two decades, I believe."

"I don't come here very often, either." Endicott knew her friend was mostly joking, but intuited Gabriela must feel a little slighted that a witch with her fashion sense wouldn't acknowledge her, too.

"Ah, but Gabriela Gaud needs no introduction." The library witch turned her smile on Gabriela, whose face brightened with pleased surprise in turn. "How is your older sister?"

"Which one?"

"The one determined to help the strangest and most stubborn beasts on this earth."

"Ariana's great," Gabriela laughed. "She's working with rescued brown bear cubs at the moment."

Salomé shook her head. "I suppose I'm not one to judge. It's not as if I'm keeping the most conventional creatures myself." And her gaze moved with affection down to a glass cube at the corner of her desk.

Endicott had noticed the cubes of varying sizes all around the library, thinking them some sort of interior design flair with their rounded edges and thick glass. It was only now that she realized a pair of salamanders were residing within this one at the corner of the desk. Broadening her senses, she noted that in fact every cube was so occupied, by at least two if not more salamanders.

"They've got lovely homes," Gabriela remarked.

Salomé nodded. "But you're not here to discuss my herd and their homes."

"No," Xandra confirmed. "We're here because of that moon last night."

The library witch leaned back in her chair, eyes fixed on the four of them through her lilac spectacles. "I almost went down to the bridge myself, but I decided to stay in bed. Wild nights are for the young."

Gabriela snorted. "You can't be that much older than we are."

"And some of us don't feel all that young," Xandra remarked.

"I'm older than you think—old enough to know what such a moon can mean." There was a gravity to the librarian's words that said they'd come to the right place, after all.

"That's why we're here," Endicott told her. "We all sensed it was significant, but none of us knows why."

"Enny's the only one who remembers seeing such a moon before," added Gabriela.

"But I can't remember what it meant at the time, or what it did."

"That's because it did nothing," Salomé told them. "Or rather, no one did anything of note with it."

She stood, leaving her seat behind the desk to walk along the shelves of the library until she arrived at a heavy wooden door. Then, she reached into her pocket and withdrew a chain of small keys that chimed musically against one another as she rifled through them. Finding the one she was looking for, she used it to open the door.

"Follow me," she said with a smile.

On the other side was a room with long glass panels in which lived a grouping of salamanders the likes of which Endicott never would have imagined existed. They ranged in color, size, shape, and notably in habitat. Although a handful of the motley-colored creatures lived fully submerged, most seemed to have the option of a dive into water contained within their panels or a stretch of mossy stone on which to lay out in patches of heat visibly radiating here and there.

Endicott knew that Salomé had mastered the magic of controlling climate, as most library witches did. Dorothea had been able to preserve the materials in the Mire library by adjusting the air to a fraction of a degree around each specific section. Filtering out humidity, mold, and corrosive pollutants from the air was basically second-nature to the woman. Though the general public had no idea what was involved with the preservation of their library's materials, there were always compliments paid Endicott's grandmother for what lovely condition she kept the place in. And as she glanced about, Endicott wondered whether most library witches kept cold-blooded creatures; it seemed Salomé's benefitted greatly from such fine-tuned climate spells.

Beyond the bright array of salamanders were three long tables edged by shelves about four feet high which ran the perimeter of the space. As she looked more closely, Endicott noted that many of the books on these shelves were much older than those in the room they'd left, and that there were also folios and files tucked tidily alongside the books.

"Is this a witch library?" Gabriela asked in amazement.

Salomé nodded proudly. "This is where witches pursuing special studies about our presence in Ember Hollow are welcome to come and learn their history."

Xandra crossed her arms. "Funny you never thought to bring us back here before, Salomé. You know I do research on witch history."

"You never had need of this particular archive before."

"I wish Mire had something like this," Gabriela murmured wistfully.

Salomé frowned, looking at Endicott. "Your grandmother didn't show you?"

"Show me what?"

Although she had been mostly direct from the moment they'd arrived, Salomé demonstrated some slight hesitation for the first time. Finally, she said, "I don't know that it's my place. If Dorothea wanted you to find out in your own time, I have to respect that."

Endicott exchanged a look with Gabriela, who shrugged. "Library witches—what can you do?" And when Endicott began to protest, her best friend told her, "Your grandma was exactly the same way, Enny."

As if she needed to be told.

"We're not here to learn about Mire's witch library, if it exists, or even Ember Hollow's," Xandra reminded them all. "Salomé, why have you brought us back here?"

Salomé had pulled a folio from a shelf, its brown exterior coated in dust which she carefully wiped away with a soft, clean cloth.

"What you're interested in is the Season of the Witch."

"Kind of a funny name for a moon," commented Gabriela.

"The moon signifies the start of the Season," Salomé told her. "It is not the thing itself, but a signal to all that the world is, for the moment, in an altered state."

"And that state is?" Xandra moved her hands to her hips, clearly not appreciating the dramatic approach Salomé had to distributing information. Endicott smiled a little; if Xandra thought this was a lot, Dorothea Thyne would've been way too much for her.

"Potential." Salomé set the folio down and opened her arms, gesturing for the four younger witches to have a look.

It was Maritza who stepped forward first, as intent on finding answers as her more outspoken best friend. Endicott recalled something her grandmother had told her, back when she was learning how to bully and be bullied in school: "Never underestimate the child who is odd, who is timid, who is not like you."

Or in this case, Endicott thought: don't underestimate the quiet witch with the foundling goose.

Maritza opened the folio and carefully began spreading its contents out on the thick wood of the library table. They all stood around, in silence at first, eyes taking in pages thirty years yellowed and older.

When her gaze finally settled on something specific, Endicott found an account of a witch who had been dead some eighty years. She wrote about disasters strange and hypnotic: a spring snowstorm that raised the hummingbirds of Mire from their warm nests in so many jewel tones that the town seemed to be under a dome of stained glass for two days and a morning, until the poor things, half-frozen from the cold, fell down dead in the slowly melting snow.

"What is all this?" Gabriela finally said, looking up at Salomé. "It seems like random...I don't know what to call them. Accidents? Miracles?"

"They're not witchcraft," Xandra said decisively.

"Oh, aren't they?" Salomé gave a smile that unsettled Endicott. There was something in her, a haunted aspect that said they were touching on something very delicate and maybe a bit dangerous.

A low tune sounded in a sweet voice, and Endicott found herself admiring its loveliness before she even wondered who was singing and why. It was Maritza, rocking slowly before the table, head bent. Her goose stood beside her, still and silent as though in a trance herself.

"She practices prophecy?" Gabriela murmured to Xandra, who shook her head. Her pensive frown was fast becoming an expression that Endicott felt an odd affection for. She sensed that Xandra would lay down her life to protect a friend, and now, her gaze was fixed worriedly on Maritza.

"No," Xandra said. "At least, she never has before. Her magic is more active, less passive than a precog's."

"What is the Season of the Witch?" Endicott asked Salomé directly, using the tactic she would with her grandmother whenever Dorothea became too invested in her own heuristic methods. "Don't lead us to the information. Tell us what we need to know."

Salomé let out a sigh. "Although you were reared by one of the more cryptic witches in my profession and I'm sure that came with its frustrations, you should know our methods exist for a reason. But," she relented, "I will do my best to summarize something as comprehensive as all this.

"The Season of the Witch," Salomé went on, "occurs once every thirty years or so. It is a time during which our kind experience unique potential."

"You said that before," Xandra interrupted. "What does it mean?"

"Your magic can do things it has never done before," Salomé replied simply.

"That's it?" Gabriela shrugged. "That doesn't seem so amazing. I mean, we all grow into our powers over time and with practice."

Endicott looked over at Maritza, who was still gently swaying and humming. The goose beside her had not moved an inch.

"It's more than that," she told her friend, glancing at Salomé, who nodded. "It's not a natural power growth. There's something...*more* about it."

"The potential of the Season plunges a witch forward to places she cannot return from," Salomé confirmed.

"I still don't see how potential changes in our magic would be such an incredible thing," Gabriela said. "If we're just talking about a boost in power, maybe a witch needs a minute to adjust, but that doesn't sound like it should shake the world."

Now Xandra spoke up. "It's out-of-control magic." Her eyes drifted over the papers from the folio once more. "That's what all of these incidents have in common: the magic isn't just amplified, it's chaotic. If a witch can't control her own spells, she is overwhelmed by them."

"That is part of the significance of the Season," Salomé told her. "But it is not the only thing you need to be wary of."

An idea tickled the back of Endicott's mind, and she sorted through the papers until she found one she'd skimmed. "This talks about the rift between the witches of Mire and Ember Hollow."

"We're getting along all right at the moment," Gabriela remarked, smiling.

Endicott tapped the paper insistently. "But this report seems to suggest there was...well, for lack of a better word, a shit-starter in the mix, someone who tapped the Season of the Witch in a way that messed with the balance of power between the towns." She looked at Salomé. "What kind of magic would help a person do that?"

Before the librarian could answer, Maritza's humming began to take the form of words. At first, they were barely distinguishable, mumbled in low, broken phrases. Then suddenly, her goose made a loud, long call, sounding five times in succession before falling silent so they could hear her witch's words:

*...And under that storm will follow
the closing of every door.*

*Her mischief of rats
Her murder of crows
She will leave bodies wherever she goes.*

*No trial but entrails
No voice but the sound
of waves of red blood lapping over the ground...*

Maritza suddenly slumped forward, Xandra and Gabriela both reaching out to catch her. After a moment, she looked up, confused. "What's going on? Was I asleep or something?"

"You weren't asleep," Xandra told her friend. "You were singing."

"About dead bodies," Gabriela added helpfully before turning to Salomé. "Is this what you're trying to warn us about? We're all going to get ourselves killed?"

"No," Endicott said hesitantly, a gut feeling suddenly coming to her. "Not necessarily, I mean. It's about the...the magical shit-starter. All the more recent documents point to that. The initial references to her are clear, even across varying accounts, and then the fallout that's described in subsequent records..."

"Well," Salomé said approvingly, "Mire may have another librarian in the making, after all."

"What would make you say that?" Endicott asked, almost defensive. She'd never had any intention of following in Dorothea's footsteps, nor did she think herself capable of doing so.

But Salomé didn't reply. Instead, she began bundling the documents from the folio. Once she had finished, she handed them to Endicott.

"It's a one-week loan," the librarian said.

"For all of that?" Gabriela asked.

"If it takes you longer than a week," Salomé replied, "it'll be too late. Now, it's time for the four of you to go. My salamanders need tending, and there are no more answers for you here."

THREE

"I'm calling Guillermo," Gabriela announced once they'd chosen a place to eat, a small corner café with outdoor seating that was, Endicott reflected, so downtown Ember Hollow that it was all she could do not to roll her eyes as their server handed them parchment menus pasted onto wooden boards.

"Please leave your cousin out of this," Endicott said to Gabriela.

"Ex-boyfriend?" Maritza asked coyly, to which Endicott snorted.

"Enny doesn't date guys," Gabriela told Maritza. "And if she did, someone like Guillermo wouldn't make the cut. He's too messy for her."

"He's reckless," Endicott corrected sharply. "Unforgivably reckless. Or did you forget that your hares barely escaped their warren flooding the last time he tried to channel his particular brand of witchcraft?"

Now Xandra frowned. "Why would you want to call a witch that almost drowned your hares? We're trying to avoid a disaster, not incite one."

"Guillermo is friends with more witches in both Mire and Ember Hollow than all of us combined," Gabriela told them, ready to defend her cousin. "And he knows plenty more beyond our combined town limits. He runs on charm and chisme, and everyone tells him everything. Trust me: you want him around when weird shit is going down in witch world."

But as it turned out, all of Gabriela's words of praise didn't make up for Guillermo being, as Endicott would have it, himself.

"Season of the what now?" he asked, settling down at their table. "Oh, do they have scones today? I really love their scones."

"Season of the Witch," Gabriela repeated, smiling dotingly at Guillermo. Had the best friends not had the history that they did, Endicott might have found Gabriela's obliviousness to her cousin's antics as unforgivable as Guillermo himself.

"Doesn't ring a bell. Excuse me?" He turned to flash their server a bright smile. "Would it be possible to get extra jam with the scones?"

"I told you this was a waste of time," Endicott grumbled, which of course brought Guillermo's gaze right to her.

"Endicott," he said warmly, "it's been too long! How's your grumpy hawk?"

"You have a hawk?" Maritza brightened a little, and Endicott felt strangely guilty for not having tried to connect with her over their odd choice of solitary animals. Gabriela was always telling her to be nicer, saying she didn't make friends easily or often enough.

Of course, Gabriela had also insisted on calling Guillermo.

"I do," she replied, choosing to answer Maritza instead of Guillermo. "He's my one and only, like your goose."

"Well, good to know he's still around and flapping!" Guillermo said cheerily.

"Is he always so..." Xandra muttered quietly to Endicott, who nodded fervently.

"It's a family trait," she replied, not bothering to keep her voice down. She could practice being nice another day. "Gabriela's sweeter than he is, so with her, it comes off as sincere."

"You know, Endicott," Guillermo went on, "I was thinking of you just the other day."

"And why is that?" she finally addressed him, crossing her arms.

"I met an old witch from out of town—he was just visiting for the weekend, on his way further north—and he had the most wonderful things to say about Dorothea! He knew her when she was much younger, of course."

"As opposed to dead?"

"Enny!" Gabriela sighed.

"Well, yes." Guillermo's smile didn't fall, though it did sag a little around his eyes. "Anyway, I just thought I'd tell you. It's always good to hear something nice about family, isn't it?"

At that point, Endicott caught a heavily pleading look from Gabriela, who couldn't stand discord and was desperate for her cousin and her best friend to someday get along. And as always, Endicott found she couldn't deny Gabriela anything.

"So, Guillermo," she said grudgingly, "what can you tell us about this moon?"

"Well, like I said, it doesn't ring any bells," he told her. "But the other thing—about the 'magical shit-starter,' I think you called them?"

Xandra perked up. "That does ring bells?"

"Sort of." He frowned. "I've heard that there was something in the recent history between Mire and

Ember Hollow, some controversy that really shook up the witching communities of the two towns."

"There's always been bad blood between Mire and the Hollow," Endicott interjected. "That's not news to any of us."

"Yes, of course, but we are typically able to keep things relatively civil—like at this table." He widened his smile, then went on. "However, there was a witch of note who many years ago disrupted that uneasy peace, and as far as I understand it, almost destroyed the bridge between the towns entirely in the process."

"That sounds...bad," Maritza commented, worry on her face. She was a much milder person than witches tended to be, and Endicott found herself feeling strangely protective towards her. Maybe she was getting better at being nice, after all.

"Ay, querida, much worse than bad," Guillermo told Maritza. "If the bridge goes, we all go."

"Come again?" Xandra raised an eyebrow.

"All the witches of Mire and Ember Hollow draw on power that flows between the two towns by means of the bridge. It's a magical channel—surely you all know this?"

They shook their heads.

"Well, the flow of magic is what allows us all to practice witchcraft successfully," Guillermo informed them, happily buttering a cranberry scone. "That's why there are such prevalent witch communities in both towns, and why the uneasy peace exists."

"Why?" Endicott demanded, not liking that Guillermo felt so much smarter than her in this moment.

"Because even as we're all trying to tap the channel in our own respective directions, when we practice, we give back to it. We can't exist without each other. There have always been witches on either side of the bridge, and the flow of magic in both directions has always maintained an overall balance." He punctuated this with a small bite of scone, rolling his eyes upwards in delight and shaking his head as if to reassure them that the scones were as great as he remembered. "It's funny how territorial we can get at times, isn't it? You would never know from the way so many of us act that we'd all be lost without either town's witches."

"But if our magic is so deeply tied to the bridge, why don't we know that?" Xandra asked. "And what does it have to do with the magical shit-starter?"

"Two decidedly separate questions," Guillermo told her. "To answer the first: you don't know because you haven't been paying enough attention."

"You're insufferable, do you know that?" Endicott told him.

He shrugged. "I am paying attention, to everyone, at all times. That's why I know things that you don't, and that's why I have so many friends."

Endicott felt like if she rolled her eyes again, they might fall out of her head altogether. She was pleased to see that Xandra seemed to find Guillermo as obnoxious as she did, though. It was nice to finally have an ally in her distaste for him.

"As for the question of your troublemaker: from what I've heard about the event that almost wrecked both towns years ago, I recall mention of a rather strange witch involved and...either she was banished, or she vanished. Funny how the mind likes wordplay, isn't it?"

"Is there any way you can remember which it was?" Gabriela implored him. "Or who you heard this from?"

"I imagine Salomé gave you more to work with than anything I might know," he said apologetically. "Dorothea would've been the other one to ask, but...well."

Endicott was not used to her grandmother's name coming up so many times within a single day, probably because she didn't often spend her days with so many other people. Even as Gabriela quickly changed the subject and their meal continued, her mind remained on the fact that the library witch of Mire was gone, and all of a sudden, that seemed to be troubling people beyond herself.

They said their goodbyes, resolving to meet again the next day and, in the meantime, look through what information they had. Xandra and Endicott split the file between them—Xandra was a historian, after all, and for her part, Endicott had always excelled at magical taxonomies. Where Gabriela was likely to get the folio all out of order, Endicott would keep her half exactly as she'd received it. Besides, if there was anything really sensitive or old inside, she still had plenty of Dorothea's librarian tools in the house.

The sun was high over the road as Endicott drove through Ember Hollow towards Mire, and suddenly, there was her hawk, catching the thermals of heat rising over the SUV in front of her. He was racing her, happy and playful after what she guessed was a good breakfast, and she felt exhilarated watching him glide gracefully above, guiding her home.

At one point, he narrowly missed a few branches and played it off as though that was what he'd intended. Endicott laughed aloud at his antics, finding herself almost startled by the sound, and she realized it had been a while since she had laughed like that. It made her recall one of the first times she'd done so after her mother had passed. She'd been with Gabriela in Dorothea's house, when Endicott's grandmother was still alive and well.

"What are you both thinking?" Dorothea was chiding them. They'd been working on a potion for a weather-related spell, a kind of magic neither of them was particularly skilled in, and their efforts had resulted in a sizable mess and no successful effects as of yet.

"Don't worry, we'll clean it up," Endicott had promised.

"If you don't break a few spellcasting jars in the process, you can't really call it studying magic, can you?" Gabriela added.

Dorothea had fixed her ever-impenetrable gaze on Gabriela at those words, and for a moment, it wasn't clear whether she was getting ready to give them a scathing lecture or prohibit them from ever using her kitchen again. Instead, she shook her head and said, voice impassive as ever, "I've never in my life heard a more ridiculous statement."

The young witches had looked at Dorothea and then one another in silence for a moment, then burst into laughter. And as she turned to leave them to their mess, Endicott saw her grandmother walking out of the room with a rare but unquestionably warm smile on her face.

Pulling up to the small house, Endicott reflected now on how it hadn't changed in any ways that someone who wasn't a witch would notice. She parked on the lawn as she'd always done, the thick grass undeterred by the weight of her car. The deep red of the door appeared brown in all but bright morning light, and the windows were framed by shutters that had never needed their light blue paint touched up since Endicott had moved in. In front of the house, wisteria still drooped in vibrant clumps, magnificent plants that Dorothea had told Endicott she'd cultivated from seeds.

"Those blooms did not come for years," the older witch had said.

"How did you know they would bloom at all?" Endicott had asked, curiosity beating out her adolescent resolve towards sullen silence. Such interest would often overtake her in the presence of her grandmother, despite young Endicott's best efforts otherwise.

"A witch knows," Dorothea had replied simply, then led the way into the house along the stone-paved path that Endicott trudged up now, her half of the folio resting under one arm and the hum of the hives filling her ears.

Her hawk settled himself on a limb just outside the windows of the solarium, as he often did, his intense gaze fixed on Endicott as she sat at the large round table where the witches of the house had always done their most important work. She carefully spread the papers out across the table in front of her, the setting sun inciting her to murmur a quick incantation that lit the candles throughout the room, as well as the one incandescent bulb hanging awkwardly from the ceiling. She'd once asked Dorothea if a chandelier wouldn't look nicer, and for her troubles had been given a glance that made her feel equal parts foolish and wasteful. Dorothea could speak volumes with a single look.

Now, Endicott would have given anything to have such a stern gaze thrown in her direction. "What am I even looking for?" she murmured, paging through the documents set before her on the table. Not knowing where to begin, she finally decided that chance would have out, and she began reading a page that happened to be in front of her.

It was a letter, it turned out, from a witch in Mire to another in Ember Hollow, dated ninety years ago. This was interesting; much as Endicott had found herself pleased with how quickly she'd started to like Xandra and Maritza, she knew it was unusual for witches across the town divide to be in touch to the extent that the four of them already were.

But was that right? she wondered. After all, there were so many exceptions—Salomé had clearly known Dorothea, to whatever extent. And then there was Guillermo, who certainly wouldn't let something like a little tension between towns keep him from his vibrant social life.

"Maybe we're less divided than we believe," she murmured, beginning to read.

If you are willing to cross to this side, the witches of Mire will be waiting to receive you. Much as you and yours might be unwilling to admit it, the records in the Mire archive suggest that this will be the only safe place once the moon is high. There is a chance that we may pass one more

Season unscathed, but why would any of you wish to take that chance? You can consult your own young library witch and see whether he has come across the same prophecy ours has.

Endicott realized that the reference predated Salomé—she was much too young to have even been born when the letter was written, never mind being Ember Hollow's librarian. And the prophecy in question had to be the rhyme Maritza had been singing; it seemed way too coincidental for there to be more than one related to the Season. Endicott kept reading, sensing that the sky was growing darker but unable to take her attention from the letter.

Whether now or thirty years from now, there will be a reckoning in the Hollow. Our invitation may be nothing but precaution, an effort that will ultimately prove unnecessary. We can only hope it will be so. But please, ask yourself: is pride reason enough for you to test that chance? And at what cost to the witches of Ember Hollow? How many of you will pay the price, all for the sake of resentment?

Suddenly, Endicott's focus was shaken by a cold grip of panic around her heart that had nothing to do with the words she'd been reading. She glanced up and saw her hawk flapping against a window of the solarium, desperate to get in. Knowing this creature to never want to accompany her indoors, preferring to keep watch from a wild distance, she immediately went to let him inside. The moment he landed on the back of an empty chair, his gaze fixed on hers and he told her through feeling to shut the window, quickly.

As Endicott put the latch back in place, she realized that the decrease in light she'd assumed was the setting sun was, in fact, the fault of a strange black cloud hovering that all of a sudden began to lower itself onto the trees surrounding her home. And it was then that she realized this was no cloud of vapor and mist.

"Okay," she murmured nervously, meeting the dark eyes of so many black crows as they settled themselves on branches, weighing down the boughs of the trees. "We've already seen the mischief, so I guess this is the murder that Maritza was singing about."

And though part of her wished those eerie words gone from her mind, Endicott remembered what came after rats and crows. Her hawk ruffled his feathers, piercing eyes fixed on the murder in a way that reminded Endicott of Dorothea. She could practically hear the old witch telling her to mind herself, to remember that magic could do as much harm as good, even to the most skilled witches.

"I'll take care of it," she told her hawk, reassuring neither of them. "The four of us will get this handled."

FOUR

As it turned out, Endicott didn't have to reach out to the others. Xandra was first to send a text, saying in her matter-of-fact manner, *I hope you're all prepared to do something about these crows.*

What in the name of hell is going on? Gabriela replied in the group chat, also true to form. *My hares are all huddled in the living room!*

I'm glad they're safe, Maritza chimed in.

Let me be clear: they're great hares, but it is a VERY SMALL living room.

To the bridge? Endicott asked, exhausted at the prospect of leaving her house again and more than a little uncomfortable with the crows darkening the world outside of her windows.

We need rest, Xandra advised. *Everyone get some sleep. We have a little over five hours until midnight—enough time for a recharge.*

See you at midnight, Maritza closed the message for all of them.

✻ ✻ ✻

"Here we are again," Gabriela said, reliably touching the vein of drama running through their current moment. Xandra nodded hello, as did Endicott in reply, and Maritza offered a small smile. She was notably alone for the moment, no goose in sight.

Endicott had not rested well during the hours between their group text and this, their scheduled midnight meeting. She hadn't bothered to go into her small bedroom, instead stretching out on the narrow chaise along one wall of the solarium. She'd told herself it was to keep her hawk company, but she also wanted to keep an eye on those crows, even if it was a closed eye. Who could know that a murder of black-winged birds staring down through one's windows would be just eerie enough to keep a witch from napping too deeply?

After a few fitful hours, she rose to feed herself and do a little more reading. Her hawk grudgingly accepted a few pieces of raw salmon from the fridge, though he let her know he was not pleased about his sudden status as glorified house pet. But to say that he was outnumbered would have been a massive understatement, and they both would much rather have him getting his talons stuck in the fabric of the sofa than facing the birds outside.

Now, bridge in the backdrop, Endicott considered their small group.

"What is it?" Maritza asked her, intuiting that there was something on her new friend's mind.

She shrugged dismissively. "Just reflecting on some of what I read in the folio, about witches from Ember Hollow and Mire."

"I imagine it echoes what I've been reading," Xandra said. "It seems like Mire might be the safest place for our kind in the days to come."

Gabriela's eyebrows lifted. "Really? Is that what the papers are saying?"

"Did your half say anything about why?" Endicott wanted to know.

Xandra shook her head, but Maritza said, "Maybe it's numbers."

"What do you mean?" Gabriela asked her.

"Well, think about it," mused the soft-spoken witch. "The population of Ember Hollow is larger, including its population of witches. If there is a magical shit-starter on the loose—"

"I love how we've decided that's to be her indecorous name," Xandra remarked.

"—then she'd probably go where she could start the most shit, I guess. With fewer witches in Mire, there's not as much damage to do."

There was a logic to Maritza's thinking, but Endicott wanted more proof before they drew any conclusions. Besides, they still didn't have the big picture of what was going to happen, or how it would come to pass.

"At any rate," Gabriela said, "maybe we should invite some of your ranks over for a playdate soon?"

Xandra and Maritza exchanged a glance. "It might take some convincing," the former replied. "We have nothing against Mire..."

"But you don't speak for every witch in Ember Hollow," Endicott finished. "We get it. No one's expecting any great coming-together of worlds, and we all know it's hard to get witches organized enough to meet up, even under the best of circumstances. It's more that Mire's here if you need it."

The other two witches nodded their gratitude, but as had happened the night before, their conversation was interrupted by unusual activity. Sensing the source of the strangeness, all four turned their eyes first towards the bridge, and then skywards. There was the moon, full and thin as it had been the previous night, but before they could take in the sight of it, it was covered by swirling clouds, a mass spreading swift as ink dropped into dark waters. Now moon, stars, and sky were obscured completely, and the night was so deep that Endicott could no longer see the others. If not for their magic, she might not have known they were there.

"Enny..." Gabriela's voice held a note of panic, and Endicott remembered how, when they were girls, her best friend had been terrified of the dark. She'd outgrown the fear, of course, but this was not like any night either of them had passed from childhood on. Finding Gabriela's hand was as simple as reaching out with her witch's senses, but Endicott realized those senses were picking up on something else, as well.

"The bridge," she whispered to the others, who she knew were feeling the same thing. It was power, distinct and dark in nature, and it trailed dread across the base of Endicott's stomach like an angry hand digging its nails into wet earth.

And there on the bridge came a shimmer of a kind, a glint of light that signaled the thin veil from their world into others that lay beyond. And from that light there extended first an arm and then the body to which it belonged, tall and cloaked, the dust of another universe resting on its shoulders like a mantle itself. The space behind the figure seemed to ripple and then still, just as if a curtain had been disturbed by the smallest of movements, nearly insignificant in its subtlety.

The witch looked through the night, void of all light but that she'd brought with her through the veil. Her eyes fell on the four gathered before the bridge, and a smile of fulfilled expectation pulled at her wide mouth.

Endicott knew, then, to raise all of her defenses. Some instinct deep within her tore at her throat, caught her breath with the unmistakable conviction that she was in certain danger. She felt her hawk, miles away in the confines of her grandmother's house, freeze as he registered vulnerability in a way no apex predator should. And Endicott felt Gabriela, Xandra, and Maritza begin to push up their own magic, the power within each of them also kindled in a protective effort.

That effort, collective and strong, came but a breath too late.

The witch who had come through the veil opened her mouth, and there extended with her breath a sound like the lowing of some dark and ancient creature not seen for hundreds of years. The sound wrapped itself around Endicott, pressed her into a kind of bubble that she could feel capping every pore, every point of exit for her own power, until she knew that there was no magic she could raise against this witch.

And suddenly as she'd arrived, the witch was gone, following the bridge in the direction of Ember Hollow.

They seemed to exhale as one, Gabriela accenting the breath with a muttered curse that Endicott was sure they'd all been thinking in unison. She wondered if the others felt as sick to their stomachs as she did, as dizzy and disoriented.

"Now what?" Maritza asked anxiously.

In the dark, Endicott felt her own gaze meet Xandra's. Neither witch knew what to say, and in their moment of shared uncertainty, a crack of blood-orange neon lit the sky. Moments later, a boom filled the air, so heavy that it shook the four of them where they stood, and a deluge rained from above. And when Endicott tried to extend her magic to cover them, she found that there was no power within her that could withstand this storm.

"My magic isn't working!" Gabriela called out in a panic, and Endicott took her hand once more.

"None of our magic is going to work," Xandra said, her voice cutting through the din of the downpour as she turned to Endicott. "She's bound the four of us. We need to get to safety."

"I don't live far, but there's a witch lodge that's closer."

Xandra nodded. "Maritza and I will follow you."

"I'll keep my brights on," Endicott told her. "The woods are thick near the lodge—stay close."

They piled into their cars. Gabriela, having walked to the woods, climbed in next to Endicott. "I really don't like this," she muttered, and Endicott knew the complaint was as much about her soaked outfit as it was about the loss of her magic and the thundering storm. "I'm not from a family that handles helpless well."

"We'll figure it out," Endicott said, trying to reassure her friend as she had her hawk not long before. "It's not just us—we have Xandra and Maritza, too."

Gabriela nodded, but the grim look didn't leave her eyes. Endicott shifted her focus to the road and the deadly conditions that had overtaken the route ahead. Navigating without magic wasn't something she'd ever done. A witch's powers were second nature, and Endicott felt she'd lost a vital sense as she struggled to turn the engine over and get the car back on the gravel. She wasn't even entirely sure she could find the witch lodge without her magic, and she could only hope it wouldn't reject them without any recognizable powers.

"How will we warn the others?" Gabriela asked after a moment.

"The others?" Endicott echoed, not totally paying attention. The storm had thoroughly soaked her glasses along with the rest of her and, ludicrous as it was, without her magic she had no way of drying them off—no tissues handy in the car, and a shirt too drenched to wipe anything dry. Her fingers were locked on the steering wheel as she struggled to see, and she felt her hawk send a pang of frustration at his inability to guide her way. Strange, she thought, that her connection to him would remain unaffected, as it was also magical. But as she searched herself further, she found that she could still feel the hives outside of Dorothea's home, as well.

"The witches in Ember Hollow," Gabriela went on before Endicott could mention the link to her animals. "She's headed right for them."

That shifted Endicott's mind back to the powers she didn't currently have. "Well, let's hope our cell phones get reception through this mess," she replied through gritted teeth, then made a sharp left and, seeing the telltale silhouette of the lodge ahead, let loose a sigh of gratitude.

FIVE

The first time Endicott had gone to the Mire witch lodge, she'd been eleven years old and full of anger at her grandmother, the state of her life, and witchcraft itself. Her mother had been killed by a magical effort gone awry the year prior, and she had found Dorothea's home transformed from the interesting house she'd occasionally visit into a kind of trap: a place she had never intended to live but that she nevertheless could not leave because she had nowhere else to go.

"Why are we here?" she'd demanded when Dorothea had brought her into the woods and taken the turn off the path towards the lodge.

"You need to learn that magic is about more than spells gone wrong."

"I don't want to learn anything about magic." She felt betrayed by her own bottom lip as it trembled slightly and her voice along with it, but still Endicott set her feet firmly on the ground.

For once, Dorothea's eyes lost their characteristic sternness for something softer, something that spoke of a pain that she shared in, regardless of whether Endicott was willing to acknowledge it. "My child, your mother wouldn't have made it whether she'd cast that particular spell or not."

"That's not true!" Her hands formed fists, tears filling her line of vision. "She should have just left that fire alone. The fire department would've gotten to it. It was her magic that made things worse."

"Her magic kept half the building from collapsing," Dorothea countered gently. "She saved dozens of lives that day."

"Then why couldn't anyone save her?" The words came out a croak, and Endicott felt that desperate, cloying grief that she hated, the emotion she'd worn like a cloak trailing the way back to Ember Hollow, though she had not set foot in the town since her mother had died.

But she knew why. Her mother had made a mistake that she would come to learn their kind often did: she'd forgotten for a moment that her magic did not make her invulnerable to the very real dangers around her. Even with their powers, witches were still human, and while firming up the foundations of a building on fire, Endicott's mother did not pay enough mind to the smoke she'd been inhaling at such close range, a proximity the spell had required. And while witches might have potions and salves to soothe tired lungs, there was no cure for her mother's asthma, magical or otherwise.

"If another witch had been there, you can be sure she would have done her damnedest to help your mother. After today, you'll understand that." Dorothea's mouth was set in its familiar line once more, and she took Endicott's hand firmly in hers and led her forward into the lodge.

Running from the car beside Gabriela as the winds roared past them and the rain soaked them to the skin, Endicott felt immediate relief the moment her hands touched the door of the lodge. The others were right behind them, and Maritza cried, "Hurry!"

But Endicott found that she couldn't push the door open. It was as she'd feared: the lodge didn't recognize witches without their magic.

Gabriela banged at the door. "Is anyone in there?"

After a few more minutes of all of them pounding and shouting, a bewildered, middle-aged witch opened the door. "Gabriela? Endicott? What..." Their voice trailed off as they realized that neither young witch had any discernable power at her command.

"Kace," Gabriela panted against the roaring wind and rain, "I think you'll need to pull us in. We've had our powers bound."

Kace stared for another moment in shock, then nodded, using their magic to pull the four young witches into the lodge.

"Thanks," Endicott said gratefully.

The lodge looked as it always had, even if it seemed considerably cozier to Endicott now than it had when she was eleven years old. Burgundy velvet chaises lined either side of the front room, with floor-to-ceiling windows interrupting walls of shelves containing candles, crystals, jars and satchels with potion ingredients, mirrors, oracle decks, and books, of course.

"A lodge is a place for us to gather," Dorothea had told a tearful Endicott those twenty years prior. "A place for witches to share wisdom, magic, and sanctuary."

"Like a church?"

An amused look crossed the old witch's face. "Much safer than a church for witches, child."

Facing the entry was an imposing wall in which a fire brightened the space, crackling as though in defiance of the raging storm outside. Endicott knew from previous visits that the narrow passages on either side of the wall led to a kitchen full of drying herbs and flowers, complete with an iron stove, mortars and pestles, bottles of rich ceremonial wines, and a witch's pick of cauldrons. And there was a grand wooden table at which every witch in Mire might claim a seat, if the gathering were large enough.

"What the hell is going on over there, Kace?" Another middle-aged witch approached, her hexagonal silver glasses glinting in the light of the fire.

Thunder boomed and Xandra turned to push the door of the lodge firmly shut behind them. Endicott knew it must have taken some effort, given how heavy the door would be without the aid of one's magic.

"Hi, Ilsa," Gabriela greeted the witch. "We're dealing with a lot of other shit right now, but before I forget: my mother wants to know whether you still have pasteles left in the freezer or if we should cook up another batch for solstice."

Xandra stared at her. "Seriously?"

Gabriela shrugged. "Believe me, you wouldn't want my mother pissed at you."

Now Xandra turned her astounded gaze to Endicott, who told her, "You really wouldn't want to see her mother pissed."

"If you need another set of hands, let me know," Maritza offered. "I haven't had anyone to make pasteles with since my older cousins moved down to the city."

Gabriela brightened, but before she could reply, Ilsa said tartly, "I doubt that me saying we don't need more food would ever stop your mother from sending some along. Now, are you going to introduce your new friends, or are we to assume this is no longer a witch lodge?"

"I think they are witches," Kace interjected gently, a questioning look on their face. "At least, they strike me as such, despite the fact that...well..."

"We're witches," Xandra confirmed, "from across the bridge."

Kace and Ilsa exchanged a look.

"Like I said: we're dealing with the emperor of all shit-piles," Gabriela told them. She and Endicott hurried to explain what they'd been through in the past day.

"And you're sure she was headed into Ember Hollow?" Ilsa asked, her gaze piercing with concern.

They all nodded, and Maritza gave a small shiver, which made Endicott raise an eyebrow in her direction. "My goose has never been by herself for so long," she explained quietly, a trace of a tremor in her voice. As she had countless times with Gabriela, Endicott extended a hand as though it were second nature, and Maritza gave her a surprised look that quickly became one of gratitude.

"Well, I don't see what's so special about it," Endicott had said sulkily to Dorothea once they were inside the lodge. "It's just a building."

Even as she spoke, she knew she was being both childish and insincere. The shelves of magical supplies and knowledge seemed endless, and she was awed by the weighty silence filling the air, heavy with warmth and potential.

Another witch, older but not quite her grandmother's age, had been standing before one of the shelves, paging through a thick tome. At Endicott's words, he turned and registered her with an expression she couldn't quite interpret, although he smiled as he spoke. "And who have we here?"

"My granddaughter," Dorothea replied.

"Ah, so this is Endicott Thyne." Something in the witch's eyes told Endicott that he'd already known who she was, and it made her feel all the more sullen. But suddenly, he took her hand and gave a quick bow, and the girl was so surprised by the gesture that she couldn't stifle her giggle.

Dorothea gave a roll of her eyes. "Really, Sebastian."

"You'll have to forgive me, young Endicott," he said. "But I stand on ceremony more than most witches in Mire. It's a habit from back home."

"Where's home?" Endicott asked, unable to place his accent.

"In a faraway country, where witches are much harder to find. Well, unless one knows where to look."

Now she grew confused. "But why?"

"Because," he said, "our kind are not welcome or safe the world over. That's why, when I heard you ask why the lodge was special, I felt inclined to come and speak with you."

"Why?" she asked again, feeling a bit thick but wanting nevertheless to understand.

"A witch lodge is hidden from all but our kind," Sebastian explained. "Even if an ordinary person happens upon one, which isn't likely, they'd never get in."

"And they'd not chance to find it again once they left," Dorothea added.

Sebastian nodded his agreement. "So you see, my dear, this place means safety for all of us, and that makes it a kind of home in and of itself. It is a place any witch can come to practice, to learn, and to meet others of her kind."

"Couldn't we just ward our own homes so no one could find them?" Endicott insisted.

"Wards can be effective, but no witch is an island—we all must interact with the world at large. Besides, you never know when you'll want the company a lodge can offer, or the protection, for that matter."

The memory of his words meant so much in her present moment, for though Endicott had grown in years and wisdom and had eventually come to understand the purpose of a lodge, it was only now, on this stormy and bewildering night, that she found she had need of the place as Sebastian had suggested she one day might.

"We should introduce ourselves." Maritza's voice broke Endicott's reverie.

"It would help," Ilsa replied. Endicott knew her directness was just who she was—there was no unkindness there. But she also didn't envy Xandra and Maritza the severe scrutiny they were currently facing. Thankfully, Ilsa had not been in the lodge on her own first visit.

Xandra inclined her head slightly. "Xandra Davis."

"I'm Maritza Menendez."

Kace turned to Ilsa, their eyes wide in recognition of the Ember Hollow witches' names. "How did this being manage to walk through a veil and strip four of the most talented young witches from both towns of their magic?"

"It's the Season of the Witch," Endicott said simply, hoping that both elder witches would understand the significance. "You didn't know?"

Ilsa swore. "I knew there was a thirty-year itch tingling at the back of my mind," she muttered. "If I hadn't been on the road all last week, I would've remembered."

"But you didn't notice the moon?" asked Gabriela.

"We've been in here working for the past three days," Ilsa explained. "You know the lodge has the tendency to buffer whatever's going on in the outside world, especially when you're working on a project. Even the Season feels muted."

"I don't know much about how it works," Kace admitted. "The last time the Season rolled around, things were pretty calm. Anyway, I'm much better with magical technology than I am with witch history."

"I'm not sure how much you're missing," Ilsa told them. "Either shit goes down during the Season or it doesn't, but it never hurts to be prepared. Clearly, if we've got witches with their powers bound and magical storms overhead, shit *is* going down this time around. How long ago did you all lose access to your magic?"

"We came straight here after she bound us," Gabriela replied.

"Do you think it's soon enough?" Kace asked Ilsa, urgency in their voice.

"Better now than later." Ilsa rolled the ladder over to one section of the bookshelves and climbed about midway up. After a bit of searching, she pulled out a narrow volume.

"Spellbook?" Xandra inquired when she'd returned.

"Reversals for restrictive magics," Ilsa said. "It's not a comprehensive manual, but it should have something that might help."

Some minutes later, they were gathered in the kitchen of the lodge. Kace worked a mortar and pestle with herbs they had gathered, and the sound of stone grinding stone brought Endicott's mind back to that first visit.

"You're leaving me here? For how long?"

Her grandmother sighed. "This child is endlessly dramatic. No one is abandoning you—I just need the night for a trip to a special archive. I'll be back to get you tomorrow."

She'd wanted to protest further, because abandoned was exactly how she'd felt from the moment she'd learned of her mother's death. But before she could speak, Sebastian turned to her. "My dear, how would you feel about helping me prepare dinner for tonight's circle?"

Endicott found that, even with the animosity she was feeling towards all things magical at that moment, she couldn't quite bring herself to snap at Sebastian. There was something irrepressibly likable about him. "What circle?"

"A witch from the city has fallen ill, and her nearest family are in Mire. They've brought her here so that we can gather and offer healing. Hopefully, with enough magic among us, we'll be able to resolve the issue."

Something twisted in Endicott's heart, then. Here was a witch, an elder in her community who had been excited to meet her and had treated her with nothing but kindness, and he was asking the one thing she'd wished someone had offered her mother. And instead of the bitterness she'd turned towards over and over again, night after night in her grandmother's house, Sebastian's open face made her pause for a moment and think: what would her mother expect her to do? Wouldn't she want Endicott to offer the help she had never received? Wouldn't she expect more of the daughter she'd left behind?

And clearly, Dorothea expected as much of her grandchild. "Listen to Sebastian," she advised Endicott. "He's a good friend to have, in Mire and wherever else you might find yourself someday."

The heat of the fire now at their backs as they knelt in front of the hearth, the four bound witches bent their heads as Kace and Ilsa chanted over them. Endicott waited to feel anything—a chill down her back, a pulse in her stomach, heat in the palms of her hands—any of the physical signs of her magic.

There was nothing.

Seeing that the four of them were showing no signs of being unbound, Ilsa nodded to Kace, who poured the steaming brew they'd made into four ceremonial chalices, one in each bound witch's cupped hands. They all drank deeply, waiting for their magic to return.

Nothing still.

•

"Well, children, you're going to have to proceed without the help of your powers, I'm afraid. That binding is holding fast, and if Kace and I can't lift it, there's not a witch between Mire and Ember Hollow who's going to be able to help."

Xandra's expression brightened then. "No...no, I think that's *exactly* where we need to go to get our magic back." They all looked at her in surprise, and she went on, "It's the bridge. We have to find a way to retake the bridge—that's what the folio keeps mentioning, and what Guillermo was going on about."

"It is where we lost our powers," Maritza murmured, pensive. "And where we saw the magical shit-starter emerge in the first place."

"But how are you planning to retake the bridge without your magic?" Kace asked gently. "I don't mean to discourage you, but you're facing something powerful and with clear malintent."

"Kace is right," Ilsa said. "This is no task for a bunch of bound young witches. When I said you'd have to proceed without your magic, I meant leaving the sister towns in search of other witches who might help you. I didn't mean sticking around to get yourselves killed."

"There is more to a witch than just her magic," Endicott said.

She remembered how carefully she'd once avoided her own powers. In that very room, Endicott had helped Sebastian with preparations for the circle. She'd paged through large volumes, seeking spells that would help the sick witch. She had prepared a healing poultice in the kitchen, stirred it in a cauldron and set it to cool as witches arrived one by one at the lodge. She had greeted her elders and made them comfortable, watched them catch up with one another. The occasion taught her that witches never gathered in sadness alone, as even a sad day was reason to celebrate the reunion of kindred souls who had been apart for much too long. And she recalled the fear she'd felt, the thing that had kept her from participating in the circle with the others who had come to the lodge.

"Would my grandmother's archive—the Mire witch library—have more information that could help us?" she asked Kace and Ilsa now.

"Did Dorothea tell you where she kept it?" Kace asked in surprise. Endicott could tell from their expression that they had not expected her to know about the library.

"Telling anyone anything outright wouldn't have been Dorothea's style," Ilsa said, and Endicott nodded her confirmation of this truth. "I can tell you one thing: your grandmother would not have kept the archive far from home."

"That's it?" Gabriela asked, her voice flat. "That's all you can tell us?"

Ilsa shrugged. "The only thing I remember her saying about it is how her bees were the best assistants any librarian could hope to have. She said they were themselves little archivists, and the only complaint she had about their skills was...oh, what was it..."

"Something about how they were more committed to privacy than she liked, or something like that," Kace offered, trying to finish Ilsa's thought.

"Yes," Ilsa agreed. "It was something to that effect, although I have no idea what she meant by it."

The four younger witches stared, flabbergasted. Kace shrugged their shoulders and said, "Library witches: what can you do?"

"Well, if the archive was close to home, and you live in your grandmother's house..." Gabriela looked pointedly at Endicott, who sighed.

"I have no idea where she would have kept it, and if it's not inside the house itself, it'll be a hell of a thing to try and find out in this storm. But you're all welcome to stay. Do you want to maybe leave your car here by the lodge so we can all travel together?" she asked Xandra, who nodded.

"Why don't Kace and I work a protective spell over your car before you leave, Endicott? Just because the four of you have lost your magic doesn't mean you need to be totally vulnerable."

Half an hour later, they were on their way, Kace and Ilsa waving from the doorway of the lodge.

When Sebastian had come to let her know that her grandmother had returned, Endicott was already awake. She'd slept stretched out on one of the chaises, the chanting of the circle having lulled her to sleep hours before. She had dreamt of her mother; that much she knew. What the dreams had been she couldn't have guessed because she didn't recall them in the slightest, but she knew they hadn't been nightmares. The sense of calm she'd felt upon falling asleep had stayed with her until morning.

"Are you rested?" Sebastian asked.

She nodded, not knowing what else to say.

"Stop dawdling, child." Dorothea's voice echoed through the lodge. "Last night, you accuse me of abandonment, and now I return for you and you're not even ready to leave!"

"I'm coming, I'm coming." She'd expected her voice would sound sullen, as it had for much of the time she'd been with her grandmother. But now, she felt there was a smile in her words and she wasn't sure how it had come to be there. "Was your mission successful?"

"My 'mission'?" Dorothea rolled her eyes. "How grand!"

"Well, you Thyne witches have always had a little taste for grandeur," Sebastian said, chuckling. "Endicott was a great help to us last night. I've no doubt she'll grow to be as talented a witch as ever existed in her family."

"I didn't even do any magic," Endicott told him, blushing a little at the praise.

"Didn't you?" Sebastian replied. "Hmm—I never noticed."

"Enough of that, now," Dorothea said, though Endicott could tell she was pleased with Sebastian's account of her helpfulness. "I have a good deal of work to do today, and I'm already behind. Come, Endicott."

As they drove through the persisting storm, Endicott racked her mind. Where would Dorothea have kept a hidden archive? She had always been working, or so it had seemed to Endicott. Her grandmother was one of the sharpest, most no-nonsense, well-read witches in all of Mire—in both sister towns, it was starting to become clear. But like any library witch, she had kept her secrets well.

They would uncover the archive soon enough, she reasoned as she struggled to drive safely through the continuing storm. If Endicott knew anything, it was the way back home to Dorothea's house, whatever the weather. They were almost there.

SIX

"It would be a lot easier to search this place if we had our magic," Gabriela complained.

"No arguments here." Xandra was slowly dragging her hands along the pantry walls, and while her movements were patient, Endicott could see the annoyance on her face.

She couldn't blame them; Endicott was struggling to keep her own irritation at bay. Library witches, it seemed, were very much about keeping order, but an order that made sense only to them. And, as the sole librarian for the witches of Mire, Dorothea had been no exception to this apparent rule.

"Where would you hide a library?" she murmured as she turned to head back to her grandmother's old room. But speaking the question aloud brought a new possibility to Endicott's mind, and she found herself trailing towards the parlor, in which there was already a small personal library. To hide a library within a library would be a redundancy, but one that wouldn't fall out of the realm of Dorothea Thyne's enigmatic sense of humor.

Endicott began glancing across spines with her fingertips, pulling out titles here and there, checking behind and beneath rows of books. Just as she was starting to feel this might be yet another dead end, she found a book that had a body thicker than its spine. She pulled it out and found that between the pages of this volume she'd never really noticed or needed—a complete Portuguese-English dictionary—was an array of photographs, along with a series of envelopes. She set the massive book down on a table and began to carefully page through.

The photographs were 1960s instamatic prints, surprisingly well-preserved, though given her recent tour of the Ember Hollow witch library, Endicott realized that her grandmother must have worked a fair amount of climate magic on the house and all the paper and books within it. Many of the photos included a woman who looked not dissimilar from Endicott herself, also in her thirties and fashioned in high boots, mock-neck dresses, and high-waisted slacks, her dirty blonde hair teased into updos that looked like they probably required as much magic as hairspray to remain in place.

"Did you find something?" Gabriela approached, and then her eyes widened as she took in the photos. "Wow! La nieta didn't fall far from the tree. She's a dead ringer for you, Enny—or I guess, you are for her."

"I've never seen these before." Endicott was looking at the other people in the photos, trying to find faces she recognized. While she knew a few from the witch community more generally, there were three faces in particular that kept popping up that she was certain she had never encountered in her life.

"Anything relevant to what we're looking for?" Xandra and Maritza had joined them.

Endicott shrugged. "I'm not sure."

"Do you mind if we open the envelopes and read what's inside?" Gabriela asked her.

She shrugged again. "That's what we're here to do, isn't it?"

"I know," her best friend said gently, "but it's still your home. These are your grandmother's things, and you're entitled to some privacy if you want it."

"We can always keep looking elsewhere," added Maritza helpfully.

"I'm okay." Catching Gabriela's eye, she allowed herself a small smile. "Really, I don't mind. I mean, if you can't look through your grandmother's private history with the witches you just lost your magic alongside, who can you look at it with?"

But the find was another dead end after all, it seemed. The letters appeared to mention the three unfamiliar witches in the photos—Basil, Joan, and Cynthia—and there was a story there, Endicott could tell. But she didn't have the spare time to piece it together now.

"I don't think this is going to help us," Xandra finally said. "Sorry, Endicott—it's interesting, but I don't think your grandmother was even a librarian yet when these letters were written."

Defeated, the four looked at each other in silence. Finally, Gabriela said, "Well, I know where everything important in this house is, so: why don't I make up the guest cots and you can throw some food together for us, Enny?"

✢　　✢　　✢

The dinner was a strangely pleasant one. If someone had told Endicott the week before that she'd be sitting at the table in her solarium, powers bound and breaking bread with Gabriela and two witches from Ember Hollow, her hawk overlooking the company from inside the house, she never would have believed it. But as they ate and the conversation flowed easily, she wondered at the fact that they all hadn't become friends long ago. She was glad for the chance to learn more about the others: Xandra was applying for doctoral programs abroad to formalize her interest in ancient magical histories, and Maritza spent her days working at an Ember Hollow daycare and her evenings teaching at a trendy sip-and-paint spot.

"What about you, Endicott?" Xandra asked. "What occupies your days when you're not chasing the witch who bound us?"

Endicott sighed. She hated this question, or rather, hated the answer she had to give. "Data analysis."

"Can you elaborate?" Xandra prompted.

"Not really." She popped another bite of asparagus into her mouth, hoping it would keep her from having to answer, and chewed while the table waited expectantly.

"That sounds like a solid job," Maritza offered kindly.

"She hates it," Gabriela told the others.

"I like paying my bills. And I get to work from home, which can be nice."

"What would you rather be doing?"

"Xandra," Maritza chided. "That's a bit intrusive."

"She just said an hour ago that she'd rather go through all her grandmother's private shit with us than with anyone else." Xandra waved a defensive hand in the air. "Why can't I ask a question?"

"You can ask," Endicott told her, chuckling a little. There was something comforting about knowing that she and Gabriela weren't all that unique, that a pair of witches a lot like them lived just across the bridge. "But I don't have a good answer. I started to do freelance data entry because I didn't know what else to do with myself and I needed money, and then data entry became data analysis, and...well, I haven't found anything better yet."

"You can always change your mind," Maritza told her encouragingly. "It sounds like a strong enough skillset to propel you into something else."

"Don't you think changing career paths after you're thirty is a bit strange?"

"I'm about to do it," Xandra remarked. "It has little to do with age. Didn't we just learn from those letters that Dorothea found her career when she was at least as old as you are now, if not older?"

Feeling self-conscious, Endicott used the only conversational exit strategy she had at the moment: invoking their current disaster. "Well, I doubt I'll get to stay in any career for very long if we don't figure out a way to get our powers back."

"I think we need to sleep first," Gabriela said, grinning as Maritza unsuccessfully stifled a yawn. "I felt that in my bones."

The two guest cots were set out in the parlor, which had room enough once some furniture was rearranged. Gabriela took the sofa, her spot of choice since they were girls. Endicott returned to the solarium, the table now clear and her hawk resting on the back of a chair, apprehensively regarding the storm outside. She briefly entertained the thought of taking out her half of the folio and combing through for more answers, but she knew she needed rest. Once again foregoing a trip to her bedroom, she settled onto the chaise.

The solarium and parlor were joined by a wide arched doorway, and so she was able to see the other witches as she wrapped a heavy sheet more tightly over herself. Xandra and Gabriela were already asleep, but Maritza pushed herself up a little on her elbows, catching Endicott's eye.

"Get some rest," she whispered. "Really."

Endicott nodded, smiling. "I will," she mouthed back.

Had they still had their magic, the sentiment could have been shared with less effort. Even so, the brief moment of connection reminded her once again that even with her powers bound, she was still one in a company of witches. And she was glad of it as she drifted off to sleep.

SEVEN

The next morning, her hawk woke Endicott with a sharp, cheerful chirp. She blinked groggily, catching sight of Gabriela covered almost completely by a huge comforter on the sofa and Xandra still stretched out on her cot. Maritza was nowhere to be found, but Endicott caught the telltale odor of coffee wafting from the kitchen.

She approached her hawk as he chirped again, realizing that the storm had quieted and morning light was coming through the glass of the solarium. There was an eerie green tint to the sky that said they were not quite out of the woods, but it was a relief to no longer hear incessant wind and rain. Endicott reached out an arm and her hawk stepped carefully on, acquiescing to domesticity for the time being. She followed her nose to the kitchen.

"Good morning," Maritza said. "Milk and sugar?"

"Please." Endicott let her hawk down onto the windowsill, which she could tell he didn't love as a perch, but he settled for the moment.

Maritza handed her the cup and nodded towards Endicott's hawk. "I'm glad he made it inside in time. I don't know that the crows would've actually made an attack, but my girl certainly didn't trust them."

"Is she doing all right?" Endicott asked gently. "I'm sorry she's not here with us."

"I know she's missing me as much as I am her, but my aunt will check on her if she can. She lives down the street from me, and she'll have noticed I'm not back in Ember Hollow by now. The first person she'd call to check up on me would be Xandra, and with both of us unable to respond with our magic, plus our phones drying overnight..." Maritza nodded firmly, as though to reassure herself. "By now, she's definitely with my goose, and my hives, for that matter."

"That's good," Endicott told her encouragingly. She glanced over at the counter where the four of them had left their switched-off phones under a layer of rice, and was glad to see that they at least looked pretty dry. Then, to get Maritza on a less distressing subject, she said, "You know, I don't think I've had a chance to ask her—what animals does Xandra keep?"

"Oh." The corners of Maritza's mouth quirked up. "Well, I don't suppose someone with a lone bird will judge too harshly..."

Endicott raised her eyebrows. "Now you have to tell me."

"Actually, aside from her hives, Xandra only has cats."

Choking a little on the sip of coffee she'd just taken, Endicott managed to cough out, "I'm sorry?"

No one kept cats. Cats kept themselves; every witch alive knew that.

Maritza laughed. "I know. I tried to tell her once, but—well, she's as stubborn as the cats themselves, I guess."

Endicott couldn't help but laugh with her. What were the odds of the four of them finding one another? A witch with a lone hawk, one with a goose, one with cats. Gabriela's hares might be more commonplace, but her sister Ariana more than made up for it with her adventures tending to bears, bobcats, and all sorts of other unusual wildlife. It was absurd to think about, and a delightful break from the gravity they'd been facing for the past days.

A comfortable silence fell on them for the moment, and then Endicott found herself saying, "You know, I didn't expect the two of you would be so..."

"I know." Maritza gave her now familiar shy smile. "We didn't think you'd be all that welcoming, either. Well, Xandra had her doubts, anyway."

"You didn't?"

Maritza shrugged. "Witches are witches, at the end of the day. The towns may have some bad blood between them, but magic binds."

That made Endicott think of where she'd been in the folio when she'd stopped reading. Tentatively, she asked Maritza, "Can I show you something from what Salomé gave us?"

"Of course."

Retrieving the bundle, they carefully moved the pages around until Endicott found the letter from the Mire witch to her kindred in Ember Hollow.

"I guess it's good to know I'm not the only one tapping into this prophecy."

"Was it scary?" Endicott asked. "Suddenly developing a new power, I mean."

Maritza seemed to think about this. "Not scary—strange, definitely. I felt a little queasy, to be honest, which I'm not used to. My magic is active and I channel a lot of it through my hands, so I'm more accustomed to a tingling sensation moving down my arms."

"That's interesting," Endicott commented. "Gabriela's magic is tingly, too, but she says she feels it more from her heart."

"Protective magic?"

Endicott nodded, thinking about her best friend's powers. "It runs in the Gaud family, along with a green thumb, although that skipped Gabriela."

"What about you?"

"I like to tidy things," she said. "I get chills whenever I come across too much magical mess. And like you, sometimes it manifests in my hands. It's like untying knots—my palms can get pretty warm when that happens."

Maritza smiled again. "See? The tension between Ember Hollow and Mire isn't anything so serious as a magical shit-starter coming to wreak havoc beneath an eerie moon. We've got a lot in common—we just need a few more meals between us, and I'm sure we'd all stop feuding pretty quickly."

"Yeah." The notion made Endicott pause to reflect. "But if Mire is the safer place to be at the moment, how are we going to get the rest of the Ember Hollow witches across the bridge?"

"Some of us managed the trip before the way became impassible," a familiar voice said, and Endicott and Maritza turned to find Salomé in the doorway of the kitchen, with Xandra and two other witches standing just behind her.

"You're a sight for sore eyes!" Maritza cried warmly as one of the witches came to embrace her.

"Well, you know, all I wanted upon coming home from clear across the country was to find myself neck-deep in chaos." The witch holding her had a deep voice, and at least ten years and a head and a half on Maritza. Despite his joking, Endicott could see emotion shining in his dark brown eyes.

"This is Sahir." Maritza turned to introduce him to Endicott. "We've been friends since we were babies."

"Since you were a baby, little sis," he teased, nudging her. "I've always been older and wiser."

"And this is Katerina." Salomé gestured to the other witch, whose long silvery hair was at first the only hint that she was the eldest of the gathered company. Though other age markers on second glance suggested that she was at least in her early sixties—deep creases around her eyes and knuckles that were starting to become arthritic—there was something joyful in her face that reminded Endicott of childhood.

"It is so wonderful to meet Dorothea's grandchild," she greeted Endicott, her words carrying the trace of an accent that had faded over many years. "And to be back in this house. There was a time where I needed help, and your grandmother was the one to provide it. Then and now, this place has always felt like sanctuary."

It was beginning to be familiar, this experience of learning about Dorothea from the witches of Ember Hollow as she met them. The odd feeling of gleaning things she had not known about the woman who'd raised her came with the comfort that much of what she was learning was positive, that her grandmother had been a friend and more to people she hadn't even known existed, and that even now, those people were thus glad to meet Endicott in turn.

"What's happening?" Gabriela stumbled into the kitchen, hair at all angles and eyes half-closed, comforter still over her shoulders like a ridiculously oversized cloak. The laughter she received in response seemed to wake her, and stifling a yawn, she looked at Endicott quizzically.

"Is there enough coffee for her?" Endicott asked Maritza.

"I always make more than enough," Maritza replied, and together they prepared cups for all the witches in the kitchen.

"How's the bridge holding up?" Gabriela asked the new additions to their party.

"We almost didn't make it," Sahir replied grimly. "Thankfully, Katerina has been through the Season twice before, and she sensed there might be obstacles building between the towns once the storm started."

"Well, not quite twice," Katerina said, sparkling eyes apologetic. "I'm afraid I was nowhere near the sister towns during my first Season, and I was very young. But I do remember mention of it in the aftermath."

"Really?" Xandra asked in surprise. "People kept talking about it?"

"That was when your 'shit-starter' entered our cognizance," Katerina replied. "People spoke of the disaster for some years, even if just in passing."

Gabriela grimaced. "No wonder the bridge is already an issue."

"We had to use our collective power to force a path across," Katerina went on. "Salomé's climate magic came in quite handy—it's the only way we were able to create passage through the storm. After she'd constructed enough atmospheric stability, I was able to tap the bridge's energies, to force it to recognize us as witches of one of the towns to which it is meant to provide access."

"Then Sahir cleared the creatures that had shown up to bar our way," Salomé said.

"Creatures?" Endicott asked, though she was sure she knew the answer.

"A mischief and a murder," Sahir replied, confirming her suspicions. "Dramatic, really, and that's coming from a witch who spent the last year and a half keeping harbor seals."

"Did they try to attack?" Endicott pressed.

Sahir scratched his chin. "It's hard to characterize a flock of crows flapping so thickly you can't see past them as 'attacking.' It's more like: how the hell would you go about getting through them?"

"How did you?" Gabriela wanted to know.

"Animals like me," he said simply. "Even other witches' creatures will sometimes accept my influence. I just asked that they do us no harm, as we had no choice but to pass into Mire."

Endicott and Gabriela exchanged a glance, twin smiles pulling at their mouths. They were both thinking of Ariana, and it struck Endicott once more how unlikely her present company seemed. All witches were eccentric by nature, but this group included some real outliers, individuals who had habits that were downright unlike their kind. How strange that they would all be gathered together in the same place at the same time—and, she reflected, how fortunate.

"At any rate," Salomé told them, "all the witches of Ember Hollow are stuck there for the moment. The bridge will not provide safe passage in either direction, I'm afraid."

"Not only that," Katerina added. "Any attempts to cross might force the travelers into the rift left behind by the rogue you encountered, and who knows what part of existence she has stepped through from?"

"You mean the veil is still open?" Xandra asked, concern filling her eyes which only grew as the others nodded solemnly to confirm that this was the case.

Before they could say anything further, Endicott's hawk suddenly let loose a few loud chirps, then fluttered his wings in a manner that told Endicott he was coming to her. Surprised, she nevertheless extended her arm. He flapped restlessly, and she looked at her companions. "He wants to head outside. Not by himself, I mean—with all of us."

"I'm not one to ignore a witch who keeps a hawk, or the hawk himself, for that matter," Salomé said. "Let's do as he asks."

Endicott saw that the sky was not nearly as dark as it had been, though there was a foreboding cover of clouds in the distance over Ember Hollow. Veins of lightning and rumbles of thunder extended from that same direction, and she could see Xandra and Maritza tense as they recognized the danger hovering directly above their home.

But her hawk led them in the opposite direction, towards Dorothea's hives. He circled low, screeching, and Endicott noticed immediately that there had been a change in the bee colonies. She walked slowly over to them, their hum significantly diminished from its usual comforting buzz.

"A lot of the bees have left the hives," she told the other witches. "More than just workers collecting nectar and pollen."

"They can't have gone far," Xandra said, and Endicott could hear an effort towards reassurance in her voice. "A witch's colonies would know better than to fly into that storm."

"Any bees would," Salomé agreed. "They have left their home for good reason, I'm sure. Xandra, you told us that you've been seeking the Mire witch library?"

Xandra nodded. "Dorothea once said the bees were her assistants, apparently."

A small smile formed on Salomé's mouth. "They would be."

"Does that mean the library's here?" Maritza wanted to know.

"Where?" Endicott asked, looking around the clearing where the hives sat.

"It means it's likely close," said Salomé. "I know a little about the Mire library, but Dorothea would not have shown it to me on a whim."

"Sounds familiar," Xandra quipped, though her tone was affectionate.

"We should search the area," Katerina advised. "Salomé is right—Dorothea wouldn't have taken her bees far from home."

"Let's work in groups," suggested Sahir. "A witch with powers for each one who's bound."

"That leaves an odd one of us out," Gabriela reminded him.

Salomé gave Endicott an appraising look. "One of you has the advantage of this being home. Endicott can search on her own."

There was the unspoken suggestion, in Salomé's words and her gaze, that Endicott should be able to find her bees with or without her magic. Or perhaps it was an acknowledgment of what Endicott herself had realized earlier: that magic wasn't just the use of active powers, and as Maritza had said, a witch was a witch, bound or otherwise. Either way, Endicott did not protest; she treated the instructions of this library witch as she would have those of the one who had raised her, and without complaint or question began her search.

It had been a long time since she'd walked around the house. She hadn't needed to gather herbs recently, or do much beyond occasionally checking the hives. But as she strolled along slowly, she was reminded of Dorothea more and more.

Before her were the violets her mother had taught her to weave into bracelets when Endicott was still toddling, on the very first visit to Dorothea's home that she could recall. Beyond that was a patch of swamp milkweed, a plant Dorothea had adored because it drew butterflies to her garden but was not invasive as other milkweed varieties tended to be. Endicott could practically hear the old witch's voice saying approvingly, "Here's a plant that does no harm and quite a lot of good." There, as she walked, were wild spring peepers, which Dorothea had once told her preferred the quiet of Mire to the bustle of Ember Hollow. Here was the fern patch where her grandmother had helped Gabriela bond with her first wild hare.

Endicott began to wonder whether there was another potential that occurred during the Season of the Witch: the potential to remember those you had lost to time, a recollection that came suddenly and radically and in ways that made a witch's heart swell as it had not done since she had lost her mother.

And then, all of a sudden, she felt it. It was as though the earth itself had begun to sing to her, to try and lull her as the sound of the hives had lulled her when she had first come to Mire, bereft and achingly lonely. Except it wasn't the earth that was singing.

"Over here," she called, but her voice came out barely audible, practically a whimper as the emotions that had overwhelmed her refused to be kept at bay.

Gabriela, walking with Katerina, caught sight of her even if she couldn't hear her. And, reminding Endicott of one of many reasons they were close as witches could be, she began to sound the alarm that her best friend could not. "Endicott's found something!"

They gathered around her, and as they did their eyes all lit up with the shared recognition of the hum of a beehive as it sang beneath their feet. The witches who still had their magic moved into formation, hands linked and facing one another, and the three of them began chanting a spell to open doors.

Off to one side of the group, the ground shifted. But it was evident after a moment that Sahir, Katerina, and Salomé were experiencing some resistance. Once again, Salomé caught Endicott's eye, and she nodded her encouragement at her old colleague's grandchild.

Endicott made her way to the space that had opened in the earth. At her approach, it stretched suddenly wide, as if it knew her. And, she realized, it did.

"You doing okay, Enny?"

The reassuring presence and warmth of Gabriela's hand in hers was exactly the nudge of courage she needed. Nodding, Endicott made her way along wooden steps leading into the earth, Gabriela by her side the whole way down.

EIGHT

At the base of the stairs was an underground room, ovaline and much larger than Endicott would have expected. It was easy enough to see, as the ground above their heads was oddly porous, full of holes that served to allow light, air, and, Endicott realized in amazement, countless honeybees into the space. There were two long tables on either side of the room, walls of shelves supported by ancient tree roots, and eight or ten stools placed haphazardly about. The shelves were full, and suddenly, Endicott understood exactly what her grandmother had meant about the bees acting as privacy-obsessed archivists.

"Is that wax?" Maritza breathed, taking in the same sight.

"They've been preserving everything," Katerina said, shaking her head in astonishment. "It's brilliant."

"But how?" Xandra asked, frowning. "I mean, what happens in the heat of summer? They can't possibly keep the brood cool in their hives and the wax here solid at the same time."

All of the witches looked puzzled, until Salomé began to laugh. "Oh, my—yes, it makes sense. Oh, Dorothea *was* brilliant."

"Care to elaborate?" Sahir asked. "I don't doubt that's true, but I'd love to know the why and the how of it all. It's not every day you find a librarian able to keep her climate control alive and well from beyond the grave."

"Why do witches keep bees?" Salomé posed the question to them all.

"We always have," Gabriela said. "That's like asking why we do magic."

Salomé nodded, smiling broadly, as if her question had been answered more than satisfactorily, which only made Gabriela's face grow more confused.

"Hives mean connection," Katerina spoke now. "Honeybees must form a network to survive, and so must we. We are always connected to one another and the world around us. It's how we hand our magic down—oh, I see."

Now Salomé and Katerina were laughing together, and the rest of the witches looked absolutely dumbstruck until Maritza's jaw dropped. "I get it!"

"Okay, tell us like we don't get it," Gabriela told her. "Because: we don't get it."

"The hives are Dorothea's!"

"Technically, they're Endicott's."

Maritza shook her head vigorously. "No, I mean, Endicott *inherited* the hives."

Xandra let out a frustrated breath. "Maritza, I'm about to leave you in the library with Salomé when we get back home."

"Bees aren't individual animals—they're a persistent network, like Katerina says." Maritza seemed barely able to contain herself as she rushed to explain. "The hive is always renewing itself, and in a way, the colony as an entity never dies."

"So..." Gabriela waved her on.

"So, if the entity that Dorothea charged with helping her maintain the archive never dies," Maritza said, "then the magic linked to their maintenance of that archive never dies, either. The climate magic and the materials in the Mire witch library will live on as long as Dorothea's original bee colonies do!"

"Holy shit," Sahir said. "That *is* brilliant."

"And that's why the door opened for Enny, even without her magic," Gabriela murmured in amazement. "As long as the bees' keeper is the one to approach the library, the door will open for her."

"Your grandmother was something else," Xandra told Endicott.

For the first time, she felt inclined to not only take in the praise, but to affirm it. "She really was." Then, worry rose in her. "What if there's nothing here? Not *nothing*, but nothing that can help us. What if we came all this way and she never happened to collect anything on the Season?"

"Doubtful," Katerina said, gesturing to a shelf nearest her. "These records are labelled with references to all sorts of occurrences in Mire extending back well over a hundred years."

"Dorothea was meticulous, as a person and as a librarian, and I don't think she would have a gap in her collection concerning an event that happens every three decades," agreed Salomé. "We just need to take our time and search carefully."

As if sharing an unspoken strategy, they all spread out within the archive, each searching a different part of the space.

"Okay, now I understand why Dorothea said the bees were a bit overzealous," Gabriela said after a while, exasperatedly holding up a pamphlet she'd come across. "Look at these documents! They're preserved, but they're also impossible to read—the wax is way too thick."

She wasn't wrong. Of the many folios and papers on the shelves, several were completely encased in impenetrable beeswax. Endicott had no doubt those materials were safely preserved, and perhaps much older than they might seem at first glance thanks to the bees' attentions, but to get them out would be a time-consuming and delicate ordeal.

As she looked around, she realized Dorothea had left blades and other tools that could be used to edge the wax off. She brushed her fingertips lightly across the handles of some of these where they lay scattered on a tabletop, and for a moment, it was almost as though she hadn't lost her magic, as though she felt a vibrancy left behind by her grandmother's careful touch as she must have meticulously wielded these instruments years before.

"Here," Xandra called over her shoulder, moving some books aside to access a folio. "It's labeled Season of the Witch, dated sixty years ago."

They gathered around the table as Xandra carefully set the bundle down, and Endicott could see how prepared the witch from across the bridge was for the studies in history she would soon take up. From stories of archival visits Dorothea had told, Endicott knew Xandra might soon handle books so old they would need to be propped up on foam supports, pages held by weighted ropes in lieu of heavy hands, fingertips encased in cotton gloves. Some of the volumes might even be old enough that their pages would have to be cut, something Dorothea herself had been trained to do.

"Do you want to do the honors?" Xandra asked, meeting her eyes.

Taken aback, Endicott replied, "Me?"

"Your grandmother, your bees," Xandra said, a rare smile spreading across her face. "Your archive."

Gabriela gave her an encouraging glance, and Endicott pulled up a stool, sitting down next to Xandra. "We seem to work best together."

Moving carefully in unison, they edged the beeswax off and opened the folio. Then they began sorting its contents, the other witches around them also sitting down to help them sift through it all.

Minutes passed, and then Maritza said, "I think I may have found something."

"You're not going to start chanting on us, are you?" Gabriela asked.

"Not this time," her new friend smiled. "At least, I don't think so."

Maritza held out a slender leather tome, and when she opened it, the group could see several handwritten entries.

"A diary?" asked Xandra, and Maritza nodded.

"What's that paper sticking out of the front?" Sahir asked, pointing. "A torn page?"

Maritza carefully flipped to the front of the book. "No, it's a loose sheet." Her eyes scanned it, then her eyebrows lifted and she passed the page to Endicott, who immediately recognized the handwriting.

"Go on, Enny," Gabriela said gently. "Read it out."

She found, feeling a little silly, that she had to clear her throat before starting to read Dorothea's words.

Though this text did not originate in Mire or her sister Ember Hollow, the witch who penned it found her way to our area after seeking connections both intimate and familial. Her name was Claudia Barry, and this is the diary that preceded her travels to Ember Hollow, where she subsequently killed thirty of her own kind during the Season of the Witch.

The diary was recovered by an Ember Hollow witch named Ana Flores, whose account of surviving the killings has also been filed in this portion of the Mire archive. Ana voyaged to the Barry home after the Season ended, where she found this diary as well as evidence of the Barry family's roots in Ember Hollow.

Not long afterwards, Ana moved to Mire and became a part of our community, finding herself unable to remain in her hometown after the devastation she had witnessed. She donated these documents to the Mire archive, expressing her hope that they would aid those in need of the witch library, as they could not offer her anything of value.

There was a long silence as they all processed this new information, and Endicott found herself filled with a kind of perplexing agitation. Why hadn't Dorothea brought her here before she'd died? Sure, Endicott had been young and a little useless, but she could have learned so much. She might have even been able to stop their powers from being bound.

"Well, I say we settle in and pass that book around," Katerina suggested. "Shall we each read a page or two of entries?"

Gabriela, sitting between Maritza and Endicott, turned to the former and said, "Why don't I start?"

Maritza handed her the book, and in her bell-like voice, Gabriela began to read.

NINE

May 29

    I took a trip into town today. I've been managing with limited groceries for some time, making due with what was in the pantry since winter. I still haven't used the last of the flour or rice. But my last hen has stopped laying, and I don't have the heart to kill her or any of her sisters for their meat—not while I have enough money to let them live out the rest of their quiet lives. They gave me so many seasons of eggs, and besides, I like birds. They're so willing to be useful.

    In town, I saw some of the usual neighbors. I was surprised Old Dr. P wasn't around, but I bumped into his son, and he told me his father passed a couple of months ago. I expressed my condolences, but when he said he'd taken over the practice and also had a new child, I found myself congratulating him. Strange, how a person can find so much sadness and joy in life all at once. I sent my best to his wife.

    The chicken farmer was doing business around town, but he told me to come back in three days. He had a few hens with him, but he's always had a soft spot for me—years ago, I sat with his son when he had a bad flu. I was young then, my powers even less developed than they are now, but I had enough magic to help the boy through his illness. Now, his father tells me he'll give me a discount that's honestly closer to thievery, but he insists.

The trip back will be well worth it, and I can pick up some more feed for all of the hens while I'm there.

June 2

There was a stranger in town when I returned, a traveler from south of here who claimed to be just passing through. Since my own mother and father died, I have not seen another witch in these parts until today.

We recognized one another immediately, his magic as visible as the broad smile on his face as he greeted me in the street. He asked where he might spend the next two nights, as he was exhausted from the long drive and didn't want to get back on the road until he'd recovered. I told him that there is no lodge within a reasonable distance, the closest I've ever heard of being near Ember Hollow. His eyes brightened and he told me Ember Hollow was exactly where he'd come from. Then he asked if I would join him for a bite to eat.

I put him off for a night, saying I couldn't today but that if he was still in the area tomorrow, I had to return to town anyway. This was half true; I had promised to come back and take some packages to the post office for Mrs. Waverly, who says they're too heavy to walk them there herself, never mind her arthritis and worsening vision.

But I would have found a reason to see that man again. There is something about him, beyond the fact that he's the first witch I've seen in an age, something I don't want to give up.

June 3

His name is John. He lives in Ember Hollow, and he's traveling to the Canadian border where a gathering of witches who specialize in persuasion are meeting to see what anti-war efforts they might contribute to.

My mother would have cautioned me against a witch such as this. His charm and charisma, along with that power of persuasion, make him formidable. But I know my mother also would have underestimated my strengths, one of which is fortitude of character. I am not easily swayed by anyone or anything. I don't fear this witch who comes from the town my own ancestors hail from, though I do want to know him—and Ember Hollow—much more intimately.

We had dinner at Jackson's pub. I arrived early, knowing people will talk and I am already considered something of an oddity, living on my own in the family home. I saw a few old women clicking their tongues and shaking their heads. They worry a man like this is planning to take advantage of a girl like me, left by tragedy to fend for herself. Eamon, the bartender, even went so far as to make his presence known to John and to check that I'd be "all right getting home this evening, Miss Barry?" I don't drink very much and am not at the pub often, but Eamon sometimes comes by the house to fix things for a reasonable price, and he's a good soul. John seemed more tickled than threatened by his protective efforts.

June 5

John has been here two nights longer than he intended, finally leaving the hotel in town to stay with me. His car is tucked away in the garage, and hopefully no one has come by to investigate, though I think the hens or my crows would have warned me if they had.

I'm less concerned with gossip than with any direct confrontation, which I've never liked. I keep to myself because I prefer it that way.

John, of course, has proven the exception to this aversion I have against company. Time moves so slowly and so quickly all at once while he is here. I can feel my magic extending towards his, and there's something kindled within me that seems like it must have been there all along, only it was dormant because there was nothing to meet it, to bring it to life. I suspect that a return to Ember Hollow would awaken this part of me further, make my powers thrive in a way they never have before.

This could be just a brief affair, for all I know. John could not delay any longer and left for the border this morning. There is a chance I'll never see him again.

But then, there is also the chance that I will.

June 9

My magic seems to have calmed since John left, or perhaps it is only the racing of my heart that has slowed to normal. One thing that has changed, however, is the number of crows I keep. Before he arrived, there were at most two dozen living on the estate at any given time of year. They are faithful creatures, clever enough to leave me little gifts and keep a watchful eye, but they've never shown a propensity towards growing their number.

When John was here, though, I noticed new members had joined my small flock, all of which were readily welcomed by those long established. Their overall number doubled in a few short days, and it shows no sign of shrinking now.

Perhaps they are concerned I'll grow lonely in his absence. I've wondered as much myself.

June 21

I had a visitor today.

John returned, asking if he might stay with me for a few days or maybe even a week if the heat didn't let up sooner. It has been brutally warm, so much that I've traveled into town to check on older neighbors who might need errands run. I try to make appearances in times of crisis; it seems to ensure that I'm left alone the rest of the time. People will mind their business when they feel like they owe you something.

Of course John will stay with me. Of course I will keep him here as long as he's willing to remain. I ask about Ember Hollow and he tells me wild stories of the witches and how they gather, of other entities and strange occurrences that happen in the town. He once mentioned witches that also live in a neighboring village that is somehow connected to Ember Hollow, but they seem of little consequence. I know, as my ancestors knew, that Ember Hollow is where the real power resides.

August 12

I was surprised to see John on my doorstep this afternoon—surprised, but pleased. I did not expect him for another week or so, but he tells me he couldn't bear to stay away. I'm sure there is some truth to that, though I am once again a stop on his way to parts north. My instinct is to doubt him, to suspect him of having a girl in all ports, so to speak. But he is in earnest, or seems to be, when we're together.

He knows that I want to visit Ember Hollow so badly, and he's starting to talk about taking me on a trip down to visit.

August 24

John left suddenly, having received a call in town. I miss his presence, of course, but it especially stings that I wasn't able to go with him, back to Ember Hollow. He said he wasn't prepared for a guest at the moment. I imagine he's from some notable family, elite witches who would expect any woman with whom he forms an attachment to be presented properly. I don't have family to vouch for me, but the Barry line extends far back in the proud history of the town. My parents may be dead, and I may not have remarkable power, but still I hope to be accepted by my kind when I eventually get there.

September 3

The trees on my estate have grown heavy with crows, and the family property is beginning to have something of a reputation around town, as am I. It's scrutiny I never wanted and that I am not certain I can easily brush away. When I've run into minor issues with the townsfolk before, I've managed some small spells of influence that have allowed me to sway things my way. But that is not my strength.

If only this had happened while John was here—his powers could handle it with barely any effort.

September 29

The town's talking about me, and I need to get them to stop.

I tried to do my usual rounds today, but I found that more than half the people I'm used to running errands for wouldn't even answer the door for me. They pretended not to be home, but such tricks don't work on witches. I sensed their presence, breath shuddering and muscles tensed, waiting for me to be on my way.

It doesn't help that at least a few crows always follow me wherever I go, but I'm not about to shun their loyalty. They're good witch's creatures, and I won't disregard them just to quiet the imaginations of those in town.

There are other ways of doing that.

October 7

I had the strangest interaction today with Mrs. S who works in the town hall. She had come across an old story about the ruin of the beehives on the Barry property from sixty or so years ago, and she wanted to ask me if I knew anything about it.

I was embarrassed to admit that I know nothing of any beehives on my family's land. Apparently, they were once quite the local spectacle, at least according to the account Mrs. S read.

I hate the idea of bees, though. I was stung several times as a child, and the memory of the pain is enough for me to avoid the things.

Meanwhile, friendly as Mrs. S was, my other neighbors are not being nearly so engaging. Almost no one stops to speak with me when I walk through the streets. I have to do something soon, or I'm sure they'll go from suspicious to condemning, and I don't want to have to do any serious harm in defending myself.

October 15

I cast a spell of persuasion today. I thought of John through the whole thing; it may be his strong suit, but I learned that I can use this kind of magic on ordinary people nearly as effectively as he does.

My mother always told me that the important thing when doing magic you don't excel at is remembering your limits. It doesn't mean you can't make the effort, but you need to sort of trick the process. So, where I might have wanted the good favor of the townsfolk, I instead cast a simpler spell to return their opinions of me to what they were before my flock expanded.

I also cast a few spells of altered perception on those who I've done favors for in the past. I made it so that my crows wouldn't be quite so visible to them. Their influence in the town should be enough that I don't need to cast any more.

For their sakes and mine, I hope that's the case.

November 2

John has come to me once more. We spent hours with one another, and I have to say, I enjoy the carnal aspects of his visits more than I'd like to admit. But sometimes I do feel like he's delaying me from going back home with him. I'll allow that to an extent, but I expect to eventually go to Ember Hollow. I don't intend to let him forget it, either.

November 18

He's gone again. He promised that next time, we'll go to Ember Hollow together. I can only hope he'll keep his word.

December 11

Winter is a dreary season, and the only time I feel what some people might consider loneliness. It is not that I long for the company of others, but sometimes it's hard to be the only witch around. You see yourself in the mirror and you look distorted, different from everyone and everything around you.

I think the barrenness of the season removes all masks and disguises. When all the leaves have fallen from the trees and there's nothing but cold air blowing through, there's nowhere left to hide.

January 29

John has promised to come back to me this week. I await his return with impatience, as he has sworn to bring me back to Ember Hollow with him this time. I keep daydreaming about it, longing to visit the place where my forebears were once regarded as some of the most talented witches alive.

My own power remains simple. I've charmed the house to maintain its grandeur—my tea is always warm, my pantry never grows mold. I keep my garden and my hens, and of course there are the crows. Their numbers continue to grow.

But I cannot hope to reach my potential living here in obscurity, far from my ancestral home where I know there is great power. I have seen John's magic at work, heard him charm taxi drivers into giving us free rides through town, watched him seduce local restaurants into complimentary dinners.

My hope is that when we head to Ember Hollow—finally—I will claim my seat of power next to him.

February 17

He still has not arrived. I would be worried, but I sent three of my crows to find him, and they let me know that he has not left home yet. I am agitated he has not thought to call or write and let me know the reason for this delay.

February 19

I have found in my mother's old journals a ritual to call back an errant lover. It's supposed to be used on those without magic, but who knows if it might work on a witch?

I know John will be angry if I attempt to use my magic on him—any self-respecting witch would be. But as each day passes and he doesn't return, I feel I have less and less of a choice in the matter.

February 23

I've decided that I'm going to attempt the ritual on John, regardless of the consequences. It has been too long, and I fear something might be seriously wrong. The crows have not told me as much—our communication is limited to the abstract, as is ever the way with a witch and her creatures—but they've confirmed that he remains in Ember Hollow, and I refuse to waste away in this house any longer.

The ritual is simple enough, and from the accounts I've read, it worked well for my mother numerous times. My power is no match for John's as of now, trapped in this wasteland without any other witches in sight, and yet I feel I may manage to gain some influence over him.

Otherwise, why would he even promise to return to me in the first place?

March 6

John has been here for three nights. The spell clearly worked—I can tell from the rush of his pulse, how wide his eyes are, and the flush that has not left his cheeks.

Still, there is some reason he must return to Ember Hollow presently, something he is not explaining to me. I worry he's in debt or something similarly dangerous. I don't understand why he won't confide in me, bring me into his world so that it can also be mine. I can help him face whatever he's afraid of. Using our magic together, I'm sure there's nothing we can't defeat.

March 8

He left last night while I was asleep. The crows have informed me that he made straight for Ember Hollow. I don't know whether the spell wore off or the anxieties that beckon him back home became too much.

I am devastated he has left me behind.

March 14

First thing tomorrow morning, I will go to Ember Hollow myself. I can't wait any longer for John to bring me there. I'll take as populous a route as I can, so that if the car breaks down, I'll be near a town where I can get help. It's never made a journey nearly so long as the one I'm about to embark on—for that matter, neither have I. But I need to go now.

This will be my last entry until my return.

TEN

"Wow," Gabriela said as Sahir finished reading the final entry. "After that, I think we can all safely guess how Claudia had the potential to become the magical shit-starter we all know and love."

"Where is the Ana Flores document that Dorothea's note references?" Katerina asked.

Endicott and Xandra moved through the materials from the folio together, slowly accounting for everything. After several minutes, they were both shaking their heads.

"There is no document," Xandra said. "We'll have to find her ourselves."

Endicott turned to her. "Now? In the middle of—well, everything?"

Xandra shrugged. "I don't see that we have a choice. We obviously know Claudia escalated, but how? She clearly states that she doesn't have much power."

"Not until the Season," Salomé reminded her.

"Right," Xandra agreed. "You told us the Season is all about potential. But we can't know how Claudia's potential manifested or how she evolved until we get the rest of the story. So: who knows this witch?"

They all looked at one another, but no one could claim any knowledge of Ana Flores. Then Maritza suggested, "Can someone give the Mire lodge a call? Maybe they'll have a record of her."

Xandra gathered the documents from the folio and one by one they left the archive, Endicott bringing up the rear. She looked back at it with a kind of fondness, as though this were a place she had spent time with Dorothea, though of course that had never happened.

Salomé walked alongside her. "A penny for your thoughts?"

Endicott gave a shrug. "Far too many for a penny."

Once inside, they finished the coffee and Gabriela placed a call to the witch lodge, setting the phone on speaker in the middle of the table so they all could hear. After Ilsa remarked that she was very glad to know they were still alive, the group was brought up to speed about the state of the lodge itself.

"Several witches have come," Kace said, their voice heavy with concern. "Some received calls from friends and family in Ember Hollow just as the storm began, but no one can get through using phones now. And because Mire is only accessible via the bridge, we can't show up in person and offer to bring them here. We're cut off."

"Does anyone at the lodge know an Ana Flores?" Xandra asked. "She's originally from Ember Hollow, but she's lived in Mire since the last time our storm-brewing friend made an appearance."

There were murmurs of conversation audible in the background.

"I wonder how many people are there?" mused Gabriela. "It sounds like half the witches in Mire."

"It's a dangerous time," Katerina reminded her. "We come together in such moments."

"No one has seen Ana for some years," Kace finally said, "but the consensus seems to be that her home is in the mountains."

"That narrows it down," Salomé said with relief after the call had ended.

"How?" Endicott demanded, wondering how something as massive as a mountain could possibly narrow anything down.

Salomé smiled at her. "Because Mire only exists at the edge of the mountain range. Beyond that is other territory—it's really a small area to investigate."

"I feel like we should know this," Gabriela said to Endicott. "Why don't we know this?"

"There is, I recall, a rich and interesting history regarding the Mire witches who used to populate those mountains," Katerina told them. "Perhaps it's something you can explore in the archive, if you're so inclined. But there have been few in modern times who would live so far from the center of town, and from the bridge."

"Not to impose on you further, Endicott," Sahir spoke up now, "but I was pretty smooth in the kitchen before I hit the west coast, and after living out there for over a year and trying new cuisines, I'm pretty much unstoppable. It sounds like we have a long road ahead, and if you don't mind us eating all of your food..."

She waved him forward. "If you can make sense of whatever's left in the fridge, it's yours to do with as you see fit."

A mere twenty-five minutes later, they learned that Sahir had not exaggerated his skills. Endicott couldn't remember buying anything delicious enough to have contributed to the meal he cooked, but she happily munched away. "You can visit any time you like," she told him, and he laughed warmly.

"It's nice, being across the bridge, even if circumstances aren't ideal." He looked at Maritza fondly. "We used to sneak across with friends and set off firecrackers during solstices."

"Excuse me," she protested, "I was much too young to contribute to any of that. I was just there for the ride."

"Should one of us stay behind?" Xandra asked suddenly, bringing them back to the present. "Since we've just been in touch with the Mire lodge, they know we're using this as a home base, so to speak. They may call with important updates, and I don't know that we'll get reception in the mountains."

"Yes, but the four of you still have no magic," Katerina reminded her. "There is great risk in you being anywhere unaccompanied with Claudia Barry at large."

"Sahir and Katerina, you go and protect our bound friends," Salomé said. "I would like some time to confer further with Dorothea's archivists."

"You mean...the bees?" Endicott asked.

"Yes," Salomé laughed. "Whatever their species, they are the guardians of the Mire witch archive. And they've taken rather excellent care of it, from what we've glimpsed."

Katerina nodded. "It's a sound plan. We can travel to find Ana and you can be in contact with the lodge if necessary, Salomé."

"How long are we thinking this is going to take?" Endicott asked. "You said it was a small area."

"Relatively small," Salomé corrected. "All things are relative, but Ana is still in the mountains where, as

Katerina says, very few Mire witches have lived in recent times."

"I legit know no one from the mountains," Gabriela muttered to her best friend. "You know anyone from there?"

Endicott shook her head, half in answer to Gabriela and half in agitation. "How will we narrow it down?"

"Let's head to the general area," suggested Sahir. "Then I'll ask the locals."

"But we just established that there are no—" Xandra began, and then understanding showed on her face. "You don't mean human locals."

"Nope," Sahir confirmed with a grin. "So, whose car are we taking?"

* * *

As the road grew steeper and Endicott felt her ears beginning to pop with pressure, she saw that the sky was brighter than it had been in what felt like ages. Their path took them away from Ember Hollow, as far as one could go in Mire, and the distance between the storm that Claudia had raised grew with every moment of travel.

"Find somewhere to pull over," Katerina advised. "This is a good place to start searching on foot."

Of course they would have to search on foot. "Nothing is ever easy, is it?" Endicott grumbled.

"Nope," Xandra said from the back seat, and Endicott could hear the same frustration she felt echoed in her new friend's voice. It was nice to have some company for her misery; she was glad Gabriela had offered to drive Sahir and Maritza, in what Endicott was considering the peppy car.

They all stretched their limbs as they looked around the wooded area, and Maritza asked, "Any ideas where we should go?"

"We passed a fox den not too long ago," Sahir said. "I could go back and ask."

"You sound a little unsure," Gabriela observed. "Is everything okay?"

"Everything is in hiding," Katerina told her. "Can't you hear how quiet it is?"

They all stopped to listen, and there was indeed a hush of sorts that seemed to blanket the air around them. This far from the center of town, there should have been insects, birds, and more making all manner of noise, but very little was audible beyond the wind.

"They sense the storm," Maritza said, and Sahir nodded, looking grim.

"I hadn't thought about that," he admitted. "I'm not sure how many creatures will be willing to come out and help, given the fear they're all feeling."

Suddenly, Endicott knew what to do. "Find a hummingbird."

"What?" Sahir asked. "Why?"

"The hummingbirds know the Season," she told him, recalling the details from the Ember Hollow document of those birds that had not made it during the snowstorm. "They'll know what an out-of-control witch could mean."

Uncertainty still on his face, Sahir began walking into the woods. They followed, and Katerina kept pace with Endicott. "My dear, how long has it been?"

SEASON OF THE WITCH

The question, though asked out of the blue, had been on her mind, enough for her to understand what the older witch meant. "She's been dead for ten years."

Katerina nodded. "And how are you holding up?"

A short, strange bark of a laugh came out of Endicott. "No one's asked that since the funeral."

"Loss does not typically hit right away," Katerina told her. "For many of us, it takes years."

"Who did you lose?" Endicott asked, her tone gentler.

"Oh, so many, over time." Katerina sighed. "There are some that hurt more than others, of course. The love of my life, she had a daughter who was just a baby when we met. The child was precious, and we raised her together—much as anyone could, at that time. We were very young, and the world was different."

Endicott nodded, a small feeling of dread moving through her. She was not sure she wanted to hear what came next in this story.

"Then, when she was not quite ten years old, our child grew sick. It was a cancer, vicious and quick-moving. By the time we understood what was happening and began to gather other witches to help us with a cure, she was already gone."

Endicott stumbled a little, overlooking a tree root in her path. Katerina caught her with a steady hand. "I...I'm really sorry," she told the elder witch, because what else could she say?

"It was a long time ago." Katerina patted her hand, as if Endicott were the one who needed consolation.

"And her mother?"

"She died a year later. She couldn't handle the heartbreak." Katerina shrugged. "It took five years to really reach me. By then, things in my world had changed so much. I didn't flourish, didn't do much but carry on for some time. But I survived."

Endicott was at a loss. What could she say? Her own life had left her twice abandoned: first by her mother, then by Dorothea. And yet, Katerina's losses seemed insurmountably worse, somehow. Part of her wondered: what good did comparing tragedies do? But then, what else was there beyond hearing someone's sorrows and understanding them through your own?

"Anyway," Katerina said, as though she was listening to the thoughts racing through Endicott's mind, "I'm glad to have met you. You are an interesting witch, Endicott Thyne."

At that moment, they stopped walking. Sahir had waved a hand to signal the group. He stood in front of a small patch of wild bee balm, and Endicott could just make out the form of a ruby-throated hummingbird hovering in the air before him. The bird's tiny body glistened in the light filtering through the trees, and Endicott heard Sahir murmuring softly to him, voice full of warmth and magic.

Finally, he turned as the hummingbird flitted away. "He's going to let the females in the area know about our search, and they will approach other males. There's some...careful avian politics that need to be navigated, but he feels that they will help us in our search."

"That's it?" Endicott asked, surprised.

"No." Sahir hesitated for a moment, then said, "I've been told that it would be appreciated if we took more care to prepare for the Season in the future, as a collective. This is a witch problem, and it's not such a good look that we tend to make it everyone else's."

There was a general moment of speechlessness, the culpable kind that follows being called out on one's bad behavior.

"Ariana always said that hummingbirds aren't the friendliest," Gabriela muttered.

"Neither are witches," Sahir reminded her with a smile. "And in this case, we *are* the ones making a mess."

Endicott knew after reading what she'd found in the Ember Hollow folio that if any creatures could speak to the volatile nature of the Season and the carelessness of witches, it was the hummingbirds of the sister towns. Nevertheless, a glint of green, and then another, and yet another rose up before them. The brown-feathered females zipped through the air, their number far more impressive than those red-throated males that appeared among them. And though it was clear that the charm of birds had not gathered happily, they began to lead Sahir through the trees towards the home of Ana Flores. The rest of the company followed at a slight distance, recognizing that Sahir was the one who had brokered this navigational deal, and that his presence was slightly less unwelcome than theirs.

But just as Endicott was beginning to wonder whether they'd been led astray, there appeared a small house painted red as any of the male hummingbirds' dazzling throats. Almost the moment the house was within their sights, the birds dispersed, clearly glad to be done with the witches who had been more trouble than perhaps any of them were worth.

At their approach, the front door of the house swung open.

"Well, at least we know it's definitely a witch who lives here," Gabriela remarked brightly.

"I keep forgetting you all don't have your powers," Sahir said, frowning. "She's got the house well-guarded, magically speaking. This is a witch who wants her privacy."

"Then why the open-door welcome?" Xandra asked.

"Because I'm old and my bones hurt," a voice called from within the house. "And I'm not much interested in getting up when you're all capable of coming inside."

They entered the house slowly, Katerina and Sahir leading those whose magic was still bound. The witch who was presumably Ana Flores sat in a green armchair, surrounded by muskrats. Most of them were sleeping happily, but a few looked at the visitors with mild interest.

"I see some of you have encountered a witch I have not seen in a very long time," Ana began, scratching the muskrat on her lap up and down his back. "I had hoped never to hear word of her again, but from the state of you and the fact that you're all here when the Season is upon us, it's clear that she's really returned."

"She bound our powers a little over a day ago," Xandra began.

"You're lucky that's all she managed," Ana returned quickly, then sighed. "I must seem strange to all of you, living up here away from others of our kind."

"To each her own," Gabriela said with a shrug, and Ana gave the first smile she'd worn since they'd arrived.

"You must be a Gaud witch. Am I right?"

"Even without the magic, I guess we're all a bit obvious."

"Who are your parents?"

"Clara and Ramón," Gabriela said.

"Of course. You resemble your great-aunt Feta," Ana told her, still smiling. "She was an odd one, always chasing some wild creature or other. You're not involved in any of that, I hope?"

"I can honestly say that I'm not." Gabriela made no mention of Ariana, and Sahir suddenly seemed very interested in what one of the muskrats near him was doing.

Xandra cleared her throat, her eyes meeting Endicott's pointedly. Well, Xandra *had* been the first one to speak when they'd come in. Endicott reasoned it was only fair she should take a turn. "My grandmother was the librarian who kept the Mire archive," she began.

Now Ana regarded her, and the smile turned to laughter. "Of course you are! How could I not recognize you right away?" She shook her head. "These eyes are getting old, or perhaps it's the mind behind them. You're the spitting image of Dorothea when she was young."

"I've heard as much," Endicott said. "We found the Season of the Witch folio from sixty years ago. It mentions an account you gave, but we couldn't find it."

"So, you've come to ask the witch herself."

Endicott shrugged. "What else could we do?"

Ana nodded. "Get comfortable, then—this story is not a brief one."

"We already know who Claudia Barry is," Xandra offered. "Maybe that will save time?"

"What do you believe you know?"

"We've read her journal," Gabriela elaborated. "The one that Dorothea had in the folio."

"Then you don't know who Claudia Barry is at all. You know who she was, and that is very different from what she has become."

Xandra and Endicott exchanged another glance. They had already waited so long to get their powers back. What would be another hour or two?

A whistle sounded from the kitchen.

"Tea kettle?" Sahir asked.

"I might have expected company today," Ana replied. "There's enough for all of you, if you like."

"Your magic is precognitive?" Maritza asked.

Ana met her gaze steadily. "Much as yours is, my dear."

The answer, or the direct manner in which Ana gave it, seemed to unsettle Maritza, who said quickly, "I'll pour for everyone" as she hurried towards the kitchen.

"I'm going to help her." Sahir was trailed by three muskrats as he left the room.

"So, you're a precog," Xandra said, settling herself on a sofa near Ana. "And if you survived that catastrophic Season, you must have considerably strong magic."

Ana snorted at that. "My magic is survival, as you're all about to learn." Her eyes followed Sahir and Maritza as they returned with trays of cups and saucers. "It has been a long time since I've had company, aside from my little pack."

"Are you glad of it?" Katerina asked, sitting down next to Xandra.

"You know, I think I am." The old witch's eyes narrowed. "Don't think you're all going to make a habit of storming into my living room, though."

There was a general chuckle at that, and Ana leaned back with a steaming cup in her hand. "Now, if you all left off with Claudia's account, my story will begin with her arrival in Ember Hollow. I was for all intents and purposes a child at the time, not yet twenty years old. The Season was about to hit us, but Claudia came just before it did. We none of us knew the destruction she would bring with her."

Ana set her cup back down. Her eyes were wistful as she beckoned the past forward and brought it before them in that quiet mountain house.

ELEVEN

As I said, I was barely a young woman when Claudia Barry followed her lover to the town of Ember Hollow. From the journal and from accounts that older witches would give after the disastrous Season had passed us, I learned that she had ancestry in the town where I had lived my whole short life. And it was that connection she felt to Ember Hollow, to the place she believed she might lay claim to, that was at the very heart of the destruction she would come to cause.

But no one knew that in late March of that year—not even Claudia herself. Word around town was that John Wright had come back from his anti-war efforts up north, and a wide-eyed naïf had followed him down.

Sylvia Wright, John's wife, was a witch of considerable power in Ember Hollow—that's political power as much as magical. She was a thrillingly attractive woman, trailing broken hearts wherever she went, and she did not take the news of a potential rival lightly.

I was in the Ember Hollow lodge on an afternoon when Sylvia came in with two of her friends, seeking to create a spell for a bountiful spring. For my part, I'd gone there to study up on clean air spells—there had been terrible smog down in the city, and we were concerned about the effects it might have on our area. As I sat reading through a particularly heavy volume, trying to decide which herbs to use, I overhead Sylvia speaking in a huff.

"If John Wright thinks he can lie to this witch, he's got another thought coming," she said through gritted teeth. "I know he's hiding something."

"John loves you," one of her friends, Annie, said soothingly. "I'm sure it's just fatigue from all of the running back and forth to the border he's been doing."

"Don't be stupid," Sylvia returned sharply. "He hasn't been up north in weeks and he's been acting like a skittish cat for the past two days. My hounds have been snapping at his heels, too."

Her other friend, Marina, snorted. "That's nothing new."

Sylvia shook her head. "I know he's hiding something."

"Well, you can't do anything about it now," Annie told her. "We're already up to our elbows in ensuring healthy blooms across town, and we haven't even started on the livestock portion of the spell yet."

A strange, eerie smile came across Sylvia's face then. I remember that it chilled me, made me glad I was younger than she was and that we'd never been in school together. I'd already encountered enough mean-spirited girls, and Sylvia seemed in that moment more foreboding than the worst of them.

"I have time to cook up a small truth serum," she began, voice gentle as could be, as though she were planning to coax a frightened animal from a corner rather than the truth from her duplicitous husband.

"You'd have to contend with his persuasive abilities," Marina reminded her. "He won't be made pliant easily."

Sylvia scoffed, but Annie added, "Anyway, aren't you worried he'll be angry with you?"

"John has always courted witches who are more than a match for his powers. He knew when he married me that I wouldn't be made a fool of, least of all by the likes of him."

At that point, a group of elder witches came into the lodge, and the three hushed their voices, cutting their conversation short.

A week or so later, my friend Helen and I had just had a cup of coffee together in town. As we stepped out of the café, I caught sight of Sylvia, flanked by Marina and Annie. Even at a distance, I could see Sylvia's eyes alive with rage, her gaze focused on a figure with her back to me.

As Helen and I started down the street, I caught my very first glimpse of Claudia Barry. She was slight, at first glance seeming younger than I would later learn she was. Her clothes and hairstyle were a bit dated, and she was bare-faced, while most of the young women in Ember Hollow at that time were sporting dramatic eyeliner and twiggies. For all that Sylvia and her friends appeared an imposing gang as they faced down this small, lone stranger, there was no fear in Claudia's face. I saw there instead a spark of defiance, and I was sure it was that spark that had set Sylvia's temper alight.

"We should go," Helen murmured, as a crowd was beginning to gather. "We don't want to get caught up in anything Sylvia Wright is about, trust me."

"But who is she?" I asked, curiosity getting the better of me.

"Haven't you heard?" a man nearby asked, smirking. "That's John Wright's little mistress, come down from who knows where to try and stake her claim."

My first reaction was shock, which had much to do with my own naivety. It hadn't occurred to me that someone in Ember Hollow might have a mistress—certainly not a witch from such an illustrious family as the Wrights. My youth and wide-eyed ignorance of the world could not be denied at that point. And on reflection, they're what saved me, in the end.

The people who'd gathered weren't all witches. Much as the ordinary folk of Ember Hollow and Mire understand that there's something a little different about the towns they call home, they are not and never have been fully aware of our presence. Up until that point, I'd never known a witch who didn't intend to keep things that way.

But all who had stopped to gawk, witches or not, were wise enough not to crowd the group of women facing off in the street, and that put many out of earshot. We could hear, of course, thanks to our magic, and Sylvia's words rang sharply in the air.

"I would leave town today, if I were you," she was saying.

Claudia Barry stunned us with her reply. "Why would I leave when it's clear he prefers me?" She rested a hand on one hip, the wind playing at the hem of her skirt where it caught her mid-calf. "Besides, this is my town as much as yours. My family comes from Ember Hollow, and it's high time we make our return."

Her voice had the smallest of tremors running through it, and I knew Sylvia had heard it along with the rest of us. The smile that had chilled me so in the lodge returned to her face. "We need a little privacy, Marina," she said.

Marina muttered the words of a shielding spell, and I saw the eyes of several of the ordinary people around us glaze over. Only witches were meant to witness what would happen next.

"You have no claims on Ember Hollow," Sylvia said, reaching into her purse, "and certainly none on my household."

"It's John's house," Claudia shot back, but that tremor in her voice had increased and I could see her shift her weight as though longing to take a step back.

"No," Sylvia's voice came in a harsh whisper. "It is absolutely mine."

When she withdrew her hand, I saw vines wrapping themselves around one another in the glow of a red and ominous light that seemed to rise directly from her palm. It was powerful magic, twisting on itself, and the trees and plants that edged the street all twisted along with it. Her words became so quiet none of us could hear them, but suddenly, I saw Claudia's face grow drawn and pale, terror filling her eyes. She bent as though she'd been struck in the gut, and then, with sight only a witch possesses, we all of us saw her powers disappear. She screamed and fell to the ground, and there she remained, slumped and sobbing quietly in the street.

"Sylvia..." Annie breathed, but at the hint of mercy in her voice, her friend turned to her with an expression that extinguished anything else she might have to say.

"Why don't we go back to the lodge?" Sylvia casually suggested to her companions, as though she had not just publicly bound another witch with a deliberately painful spell. It was one of the cruelest displays of magic I had ever seen.

Marina muttered another few words, and I saw the faces of the crowd around me return to normal and take in the sight of the crying Claudia.

"Well, it's what we all expected, am I right?" said the man who'd spoken to us before, and I realized that all those gathered believed that the spat had ended with Sylvia the victor through sheer force of her words. And, in a way, that was the truth.

The crowd lost interest and Helen began to depart with the rest, but still shocked over all I'd seen, I lagged behind.

"Come on," she urged.

"I..." My voice trailed off. Why was I lingering? Why couldn't I look away?

"Are you planning to stay and help her?" Helen asked, but I found I still couldn't answer. She shrugged. "Well, I need to go."

Alone, I found I was self-conscious, standing there staring, so I wandered back into the café and ordered a small espresso. I sat by the window and murmured a spell so I could hear through the glass, because as I was settling on a stool and Claudia was picking herself slowly up off the ground, an elderly witch approached her.

"My dear," he said, reaching out a trembling hand to help her stand, "I'm so very sorry for you."

Her face was stricken, and I wondered whether she was in shock. She didn't seem able to reply.

"You know," the old man went on, "in a few days, a very special moon will rise in the sky, one that only comes around every thirty years. Do you know what moon I mean?"

Claudia's eyes seemed finally able to focus, and she looked at the man and shook her head. He gave her an encouraging smile.

"Come sit with me." The older witch brought her to a bench that was dangerously close to where I sat watching through the window, and I had the urge to turn and quickly head out the back exit of the café. But whatever curiosity, morbid or otherwise, had taken hold of me still held me firmly in its grasp.

Neither of them so much as glanced my way, however. I don't know how cognizant of the world around her Claudia even was at that moment. Those of you contending with bound powers know how disorienting the experience of losing access to one's magic can be. At that point, I also noticed a few crows had settled into the branches of a tree above the bench where they sat. I wondered whether they belonged to Claudia or the old man.

"This moon will mark the Season of the Witch," he began, and he explained to her in so many words what that meant. Distant confusion filled her eyes as he spoke, and he saw it and said, "You're wondering what this has to do with you?"

Claudia nodded mutely.

"Well, my child, there is a way to get your magic back," he said. "But it is not without great risk. You must listen closely if you are to get it right and not wreak havoc on yourself and all those around you. Do you understand?"

Her eyes widened at his words, and she seemed to focus on him for the first time. I felt my own breath draw in; I knew of no way to unbind a witch.

"When that moon rises, you must go to the bridge that connects this town to the next. Do you know of Mire?"

"No." Claudia seemed to have found her voice again. "Is it as powerful as Ember Hollow?"

The man's eyes grew yet more pitying, and I could tell he believed her question came from fear, from wondering if there were witches in this other town who, too, might do her harm. There was something in Claudia's manner that gave me pause at her words, though. I did not linger on it as their conversation continued. Later, her question would rise in my mind as the first of several warnings of what was to come.

"There are far fewer witches in Mire," he told her, patting her hand. "You have nothing to fear there. But the bridge between the towns is a place of great power. If you go there under the full moon that marks the Season, you will encounter the veil between worlds."

"But without my magic..."

"Every witch carries within her a magical potential that is irrevocable. Yes, your powers have been bound, but do not doubt that you are still very much a witch."

"I don't doubt it," she answered quickly, almost to herself. Then she looked at him imploringly. "But how can this bridge reverse the binds on me?"

"You must, with the utmost care, place your hands upon the veil. Bound or not, your magical potential will respond to the energy there at first contact. And it will react to you, as well, should you draw on it."

Claudia's eyes grew wider still, and I wondered at how the older witch didn't see in her what I was increasingly unable to deny: a hunger, a desire that I knew could bring about nothing good.

"This, my dear, is the most important part, so listen well." He waited for her fervent nod of agreement before he continued. "Use that energy of the veil to break the binds on your powers. You will be fully restored and recover all your abilities as a witch. But under no circumstances should you remain in contact with the veil once the binds are broken. You *must* release your hands immediately, and whatever you do, do not push too hard against the veil."

"Why?" Claudia asked. "Would it kill me?"

Still intent on comforting this apparent victim of Sylvia's cruelty, he assured her, "This process is sound. You must trust that it will restore your magic."

"But if I push too hard?"

"You would gain more power than any witch alive needs. Worse, you'd chance tearing the veil itself."

I felt myself grow tense at his words. Again, there was something about Claudia's manner, injured though she was, that made me fear his knowledge had come to someone it shouldn't. I was a little ashamed, thinking that I should only have sympathy for this woman who had been so brutally struck down, and by a witch I didn't care for all that much myself. But that nagging sense of dread, something I now know was informed by my own precognitive powers to come, made me decide right then that I would go to the bridge and see what happened.

As Claudia offered gratitude to the old witch and began to take her leave, I caught a flash of movement across the way. I saw that Annie hadn't left as I'd thought, but had stayed behind and heard everything the old witch said, just as I had. My anxiety grew, and I knew I'd have to be twice as careful to go unseen on the night the Season's moon rose, for it was evident that I wouldn't be the only witch to follow Claudia Barry into the woods.

I waited with trepidation for the Season to arrive. I worried I might not recognize it, but of course, you all know that moon is something we cannot easily miss. On the night it rose, I felt the pull of its significance in my blood, felt all of the potential that would be drawn on in the days that would follow. We all change with the Season, whether we know it or not. For me, that change would be the ability to know things that were to come, a kind of instinctive magic I had never manifested before.

I chose to hide on the Mire side of the bridge. I assumed, rightly, that Claudia would approach from Ember Hollow. I shielded myself magically, having gone into Mire as soon as the moon was visible, before the sun had even fully set. I was settled safely on the ground beneath a great sugar maple when she finally appeared on the bridge.

I noted, as I had earlier in the week, the presence of several crows up above. Corvids are wonderful birds for witches to keep, clever and loyal, but I saw that they were not the only creatures to have followed Claudia to the bridge. At her heels was a gathering of rats, not quite a full mischief, but at least a few families. That struck me as odd; it's not typical that a witch will find new creatures so far from home, and had they been hers all along, I almost certainly would've seen them on the day Sylvia bound her. As I thought on it, I remembered Claudia saying that Ember Hollow had once been home to her family. The sight of the rats made me wonder how deep our ancestral roots might tend to grow.

I had hidden myself well enough. Never once did Claudia's eyes drift in my direction as I crouched beneath the tree. My muskrats had all chosen to remain behind—they're not much for wandering far from home, and besides, I needed to keep myself as quiet and small as I could. A handful of my bees had come with me, though; when I'd mentioned my plans as I'd checked on my hive that week, I'd received a buzz of concern in response. And as I'd walked through the woods under the Season's rising moon, I found I had something of a tiny security detail hovering in the air above me.

The moon grew brighter against the darkening sky, and I felt its influence where I sat, working on me as it works on every one of our kind. Then, I could see the veil move on the bridge as it responded to Claudia's presence. It was as though a wind had blown a curtain that hung within the fabric of reality itself. Slight distortions echoed with its movement, rippling across all I could see: the bridge, the trees around it, and Claudia's face and form. She saw it as clearly as I did, and with trembling arms, she slowly drew up her hands.

The binds on her magic suddenly seemed to glow, illuminated in the night, looking like so many vines wrapped tightly over her entire body. Then, it was as if something were heating and then scorching the vines so that they began to shrivel and fall away. Her eyes flickered with discomfort and she gritted her teeth, and I knew the process must be painful. But before it could finish, a voice called out, "Why bother getting your magic back when I am going to drive you from this town the moment you do?"

It was Sylvia, of course. She had approached the bridge from the Ember Hollow side, just as Claudia had. The last of the vines fell away as she took her first step onto its stone base, but Claudia did not disengage as the old witch had told her to. Instead—and her face twisted in agony as she made the choice—she began to push harder against the veil.

"What do you think you're doing?" Sylvia snapped.

I found myself whispering, "Don't, don't."

But Claudia pushed forward. I saw her face drain of blood in the moonlight, saw her gasp and seize as the pain seemed to spread throughout her body. The crows above began to circle and cry warnings, and the rats squealed as they scurried around the bridge, careful to avoid the veil and their witch even as they frantically tried to draw her from where she stood. But still, she would not let go.

Then, a sudden stillness seemed to swallow everything around the bridge for a moment. The hush was as complete as it was immediate, taking the voices of murder and mischief alike; they were all of them suspended as the rippling veil met with Claudia's last push and finally, fatefully split.

The rift looked just like you'd imagine a rip in a curtain might; it was subtle, the veil on either side of it still moving in a manner that only someone with magic could perceive. But then a boom of power shook the earth and broke the silence around us, and both witches were thrown several feet in opposite directions. Had I not been protected by the maple at my back, I too would likely have gone flying. My bees, however, were killed instantly by the surge. Bees die for their hive and their witches all the time, and yet the shock of the thing made their deaths particularly cruel, bitter in a way I still can't quite explain. My heart ached as I felt them go, seeming to sound a warning in their wake.

Sylvia got to her feet first. "You fool," she said hoarsely as she approached Claudia. "You absolute fool of a witch, what have you done?"

I had been under that moon long enough now to feel the full dread of what was to come. I retched and gagged, unused to this new sensation in my gut. The Season had arrived, and I had gone from having simple, ordinary magic to being a fully developed precognitive witch, and I saw the attack before I could even think to intervene. But with that sight came the knowledge that I could not have stopped Claudia even if I'd had the time, and instead, I doubled the concealment I had placed upon myself, barely daring to whisper an incantation as terror coursed through my limbs.

As Sylvia came to stand over Claudia, the fallen witch suddenly sat bolt upright and grabbed both of Sylvia's wrists. I could see her begin to bind her rival, Sylvia's eyes widening in disbelief followed by pain as the magic took hold. But then came the shift, and I watched as her power began to flow out of her body and into the hands that gripped her.

The whole of the awful scene took so little time to unfold that had I turned my head for even a few moments, I would have missed it. One second, Claudia was pulling herself to her feet, fingers locked around Sylvia's arms; the next, Sylvia's body fell to the ground, dead without her magic and shriveling into a rotted thing with the haste in which her life had been taken.

The power that now coursed through Claudia was horrible to behold. I'd never seen anything so hideous, the moonlight hitting her face as a deranged, wide grin spread across her features. She glowed just like that moon, stunning and deadly, and she slowly began to walk through the woods in the direction of Ember Hollow. Summoned by her burst of new power, dozens of crows gathered above her, and rat after rat trailed in her footsteps.

And just as I'd known what fate was to befall Sylvia, I knew that Claudia was not yet finished with the witches of her ancestral home.

TWELVE

As the witches of both towns were soon to discover, and as you all must understand as I tell you this now, the power Claudia Barry had gained from her prolonged contact with the veil would come to manifest as a problem with three faces.

First, there was the hunger that she now felt for more magic, far more than any one witch could require, as I'd heard the old man tell her outside the café. It was that hunger which drove her towards Ember Hollow, seeking more like Sylvia who could act as a supply for her sudden insatiable need.

Then, there was the fact that, with each witch she killed, Claudia became a more effective hunter of her own kind. By the time the witches in Ember Hollow had finished their morning coffee on that fateful first day of the Season, she was already twice as powerful as she'd been before Sylvia had bound her.

And finally, there was the problem of the veil itself. Torn as it was, and with the magic of the Season flowing full and strong, it threatened the very foundations of both Mire and Ember Hollow. There was no telling what might fall into the tear, never mind what might emerge from it. And the stability of this realm was, of course, shaken by a rift in the fabric of our reality.

Luckily for those of us who hailed from that supposedly more prestigious of the sister towns, the witches across the bridge were not going to sit back and watch as an errant daughter of Ember Hollow burned all the magic among us to the ground. At least, not the ones that I was about to meet.

After I had regained control of my body enough to stop shaking, I first tried to cross the bridge and head towards home. But I found myself choking on the stink of atmosphere emanating from the rift, and besides, I was too frightened to cross. That new power I had suddenly manifested was also pulling me back, telling me that home was in fact the wrong direction. So, though I was shamefully unfamiliar with the town that bordered my own, I turned around and went in search of help.

Led totally by magical instinct, I remember thinking that surely my newfound precognition would bring me to a witch lodge. Instead, after a very long walk during which I tried to get the nausea my new powers were causing under control, I found myself drawn to a queer little house with light blue shutters surrounded by wisteria, the humming of its hives just loud enough to reach my ears.

Upon my approach, Dorothea Thyne stepped out from behind the red front door, took one look at me and clicked her tongue, the sternest of looks on her face. "Aren't you the sorriest thing I've seen dragged across that bridge in what feels like an age!"

"How do you know where I'm from?"

She continued looking at me shrewdly. "Let's call it a knack you develop in my profession."

"What profession is that?" I didn't actually care about her answer. I was a little in shock, still feeling sick, and my questions were as much babble as anything else.

Dorothea smiled for the first time. "Come inside. I've already got my morning pot brewing, and there's plenty to go around."

A pair of hedgehogs waddled past me as I went into the house, and I sensed the presence of several more. There's something about the creatures we keep that's grounding, and after the loss of my bees, these two prickly critters were a welcome sight.

Dorothea was a woman very much of the times, the inside of the small house covered in pea green wallpaper featuring mustard yellow and burnt orange flowers. She had wooden sofas and armchairs that cradled gold velour cushions, and the brown shag carpets were clearly favored by her hedgehogs, who had made visible nests in them here and there.

I marveled at a Mire witch so modern, so in touch with the world. Eventually, as I finally got to know the town over time, I became deeply ashamed of that pretension. Now, I can only laugh at my young and foolish judgments. I'm sure Dorothea would have laughed at me, as well, had I ever told her of my first thoughts upon entering her home.

Even then, though, I was observant enough to realize that she was no ordinary witch. I'd noticed that all of the low coffee tables that broke up the space of the house were covered in stacks of books and papers, as were spare surfaces like shelves and the top of the television set. There were more volumes scattered about than even the more scholarly of our kind tended to have in their homes.

"You're a librarian, aren't you?" I asked once she'd settled me in her solarium.

"I am." She considered me thoughtfully. "Why don't you go ahead and tell me what has you so frightened?"

I hadn't realized my terror was transparent, that it would be so easy to read me at a glance. But after what I'd witnessed, I now marvel that I made it to that house at all. It was the change the Season had induced that saved me, even as the Season had caused all this havoc to unfold in the first place.

Dorothea, as many of you know, was strangely easy to confide in. Her manner was stern, unyielding, and yet I felt I had found a true friend. I told her of all that I'd witnessed under that moon. I didn't yet know the extent of the damage Claudia would cause, but I could recount the last I'd seen of her from the other side of the bridge.

"And you're sure you saw her heading back towards town? She wasn't going further into the woods?"

"Why wouldn't she go back to town?"

Dorothea frowned. "I have a hunch, but I want to be wrong. Why was Sylvia in the woods?"

I'd told her this. "Because she knew Claudia would be there."

She shook her head. "No, Ana—how did Sylvia come to know where Claudia would be?"

"Well, Annie must have told her." Then I realized with a start what she meant. "You don't think..."

"Annie was a friend of Sylvia's?"

"Yes."

"A good enough friend that she might go with Sylvia into the woods? Maybe even stand watch not far from the bridge?"

I nodded. "But isn't there the chance that Claudia only killed Sylvia because she'd been threatened? Isn't it possible she won't kill anyone else as long as they don't confront her or frighten her in any way?"

Dorothea's face was grim. "A power like that, unnatural and enhanced by the magic of the Season, will not be sated by a single act of violence." She held my gaze. "I think you of all people know how bad this is going to be."

"What can we do?" I asked, more than a little helplessly.

"We can go into Ember Hollow and stop her."

Much as I liked Dorothea, at those words, I balked. "Stop her? Haven't you heard anything I've said?"

"Of course I have," she said, sipping her tea. "Do you think we should leave her to her own devices instead?"

"But...I mean, much as my new senses might be a little helpful, we..." I sighed, unable to find a polite way to phrase what I needed to ask. "Are you sitting on a good deal more power than I can see by looking at you or something?"

"No," she chuckled. Then a light came into her eyes. "But Mire might well be—a more *useful* power than we have between us, that is."

She stood and began packing a small bag. It was clear we wouldn't be staying in the house, and I almost felt like sulking. I'd only just started to sense my pulse returning to normal; the last thing I wanted to do was go off after the most terrifying witch I'd ever encountered.

"Now, before we head into Ember Hollow, we'll make a quick stop in the mountains."

"The mountains?" I echoed doubtfully, as I'm sure some of you must have when you set off in search of me and this story.

Dorothea nodded and said, "I'm afraid I've got a bit of a lead foot. Do you want any crackers?"

"Crackers?"

"Saltines, in case you get queasy from the drive." She didn't wait for me to answer, grabbing a canister and pulling a wax sleeve from it which she added to her bag.

As was the case with her house, Dorothea's car was very much of the moment. It was a boat of a thing, nothing like you'd find on the road now, and she had not been exaggerating in the slightest about her driving skills. Had the road into the mountains been paved a little better, and had I not already been battling the queasiness my new powers had induced, I might have made it without needing the crackers, but that wasn't the case.

At that time, a handful of witches made their homes in this part of Mire. When Dorothea and I walked up the path to a small cottage, I don't know what I expected. But when a stunning witch who looked like he could've been a relative of both Paul Newman and Rock Hudson came striding out to meet us, I have to say that I fully felt the limits of my new precognitive abilities. It took me half a minute just to pick my lower jaw up off the ground.

"Dorothea," the man said, an eyebrow raised in my direction. "What's the trouble?"

"Trouble?" I managed to remove my gaze from this walking, talking work of art to glance at Dorothea. "Can he glimpse the future, too?"

The man laughed, and Dorothea afforded me one of her wry smiles. "I don't come calling on Raúl often, I'm afraid."

"Only when there's trouble," he repeated. "So what is it?"

Dorothea did the bulk of the talking. I'd recovered from my first sight of Raúl, and the feeling that we were about to attempt something that was as dangerous as it was impossible had returned to me. By the time she'd finished, I could see I wasn't the only one having doubts.

"I don't know about this." He ran a hand through his hair. "Seems like the stakes are higher than I like, and besides, who's to say our help will be well received?"

"This witch has harnessed the power of the Season, torn the veil, and threatened both towns," Dorothea replied. "They'll receive us."

"And when was the last time an Ember Hollow witch went out of their way to help one of ours?" he shot back, but I noticed he was closing his front door behind him.

"There are saltines in the car," Dorothea told him cheerfully as we made our way back down the path.

The area around the bridge was stranger than it had been when I'd left it, and I didn't understand at first how. We'd pulled over in a clearing and gone ahead on foot, but when the bridge came into view, I suddenly found myself nauseated again, and it had nothing to do with precognition. It was as though the air around us was pressurized, the way it might be in the cabin of an airplane.

"You going to be all right, kid?" Raúl asked me, not unkindly. I noticed he had a line of sweat dripping down his forehead, but he didn't look nearly as ill as Dorothea, who I guessed was about as green as I was.

"Damn, but it's a hell of a thing," she muttered, clutching at her abdomen. "Can you spare us some cover?"

"I'll try," Raúl replied, and then I realized why Dorothea had insisted we bring him along.

Never before had I encountered dampening magic quite like Raúl's, and I haven't again since. He had the ability to turn down the effects of preternatural power, a kind of magic that is both rare and underappreciated among witches. We tend to only think about turning the volume up, so to speak; no one recognizes how useful it might be to instill a calm against a storm. As his power swept out around us, I felt my tongue grow less large in my mouth, felt the queasiness subside—not completely, but enough that I could take in the sight before us.

The tear Claudia had made in the veil was visible, its edges crackling with a kind of scorched energy. It was like a wound, but instead of recoiling at our approach, the energy seemed to beckon.

"Do you both feel that?" I whispered anxiously.

"Feel it?" Raúl replied through a clenched jaw. "I can barely keep it off of us."

Dorothea took both our hands and I felt her magic drawing us to her. "We just need to push across without touching it. One foot in front of the other, and we'll be there before you know it."

It was the slowest walk I've ever made. We practically crawled across, the rift pulling at us as we fought to step towards Ember Hollow. When we finally got to the other side, that same energy seemed to release us reluctantly, leaving trails of influence shivering down our spines.

The woods on the Ember Hollow side of the bridge were quieter than Mire had been, and for the first time in my life, my town did not quite feel like home. I noted stray crows in the trees above, and squeezed Dorothea's hand, afraid to indicate them with more than my gaze.

"I've noticed," she said quietly. "Don't worry—the library isn't too far."

"The library?" I asked in surprise.

"Where did you think she'd take us?" Raúl's eyes gave the first hint of humor I'd seen from him. "Library witches love to consult one another."

"Can I help it if my new profession happens to be a particularly collaborative one? Besides, Luciano will receive us with more kindness than we might get elsewhere, at least without his help."

She wasn't wrong, I knew. Much as Ember Hollow needed all the help it could get with Claudia at large, few witches would be willing to admit it, especially to two of our kind from across the bridge. Back then, old grudges and snubs would win out much more than they might today.

I chose instead to focus on something else Dorothea had said. "Your new profession?"

"I've only been a librarian for a few years," she confirmed.

"What did you do before?"

"Oh, this and that."

Raúl snorted and she shot him a sharp look, but he said to me conspiratorially, "Don't let her fool you. She and her current role were meant to be."

And of course, you all know that to be true.

Perhaps it was because the journey across the bridge had been so laborious and fraught, but Dorothea was right—we were at the Ember Hollow library before I knew it. It wasn't one of my favorite haunts; I preferred the lodge for my own research, mostly because I liked the bustle of other witches working and collaborating around me. Libraries were too quiet for my tastes, especially back then.

I trailed behind Dorothea and Raúl. I was still lost in thoughts of all that I'd witnessed, the reality of Sylvia's death and the knowledge that we had entered the town in which Claudia was aiming to murder our kind without discrimination. And there continued to be crows visible in the trees, even around the entrance to the library.

"Don't lag," Dorothea's voice came from ahead, and I hastened up the steps of the library, where she and Raúl waited.

Two ferrets scurried over my feet the moment I stepped inside. I smiled down at them, wondering how the library remained in any kind of order with such creatures running around.

"I'm up here," came a voice from the front of the room, followed by the sounds of papers and books falling to the floor. The ferrets made straight for the ruckus, joined by three more of their kind, and I looked around and realized that the library wasn't in particularly good order at all.

"Is it usually this messy?" I whispered.

"It's your library," Raúl replied, looking at me quizzically. "Why don't you know?"

"He's a fabulous archivist, but frequently overwhelmed by projects," Dorothea murmured softly. "His new assistant must be helping, though—it's in a much better state than the last time I was here."

We found Luciano half-buried under a large mass of papers, glasses askew and tie at odd angles. He was a mild-mannered man in his late fifties. I had met him a handful of times, but hadn't gotten to know him all that well. When he glanced up at us, adjusting his glasses, the cloud on his expression lifted.

"Dorothea, my word—I didn't expect to hear from you for at least another few months."

"Unfortunately, I'm not here on archival business."

Luciano's smile faded once more, and he seemed to notice me and Raúl for the first time. "What's happened?"

By the time we'd gotten through everything, he was on high alert.

"We must go to the lodge," he insisted. "There won't be a moment to spare."

"We just made it here," Raúl complained, his gaze on Dorothea once again. "Why is it I'm always dragged all over the map when I'm enlisted by you?"

"Oh, don't blame Dorothea," Luciano told him, his air apologetic. "If there's red tape to be plastered about, the witches of Ember Hollow will be the ones waiting with the adhesive. You wouldn't have gotten anywhere near the lodge without finding me first."

Even though I instinctively felt defensive, I wondered if Luciano might not be wrong. We were in this mess to begin with because Claudia felt there was something notable about Ember Hollow, something that was hers by lineage to claim. And as Raúl had said: were the situation reversed, there might not be two witches from Ember Hollow willing to go to such lengths as he and Dorothea were in order to help Mire. Then again, perhaps I could count myself as one witch who would.

The lodge was full, as expected, but when we four stepped inside, the bustle dropped to an almost immediate hush. I felt more alienated from my home than ever, meeting the unwelcoming gazes of my community, and I was glad for my companions, that I wasn't facing this crowd alone.

Finally, Elena, a witch who often organized larger gatherings at the lodge, spoke. "Luciano? Can you explain your company?"

I expected Luciano to hedge or stammer, or even overexplain as I would have in response to such a frosty greeting. But then I began to understand why Dorothea held her colleague from across the bridge in such high regard.

"I don't know that the two witches from Mire who've risked the tear in the veil in order to save all our necks need explanation," he said. "Nor does one of our own who was wise enough to seek out their assistance."

"Ember Hollow has the situation under control." This came from Bette, a witch only slightly older than I was who I honestly hadn't liked all that much even before this interaction. She was often superior in her manner and her opinions, and today was clearly not to be an exception.

But now Raúl entered the conversation. "Really? You have it under control? And how many dead do you count since dawn?"

Murmuring began to fill the room, and Elena glanced around and called over the noise, "All right. We may not have asked for help, but it's here." She looked at the four of us, evaluating, and added, "And perhaps that's not a bad thing."

"My," Dorothea said, not bothering to lower her voice, "we almost sound welcome."

"Some of us have lived long enough to appreciate assistance in good faith, even if it wasn't asked for."

Everyone turned to see who had spoken from the back of the gathered crowd. I didn't recognize the elderly witch who stepped forward, but from the way the other witches moved aside to let her through, it was clear several of those present felt great respect for her.

"Margaret," Luciano said warmly, "it's good to see you. You always offer perspective."

"Live as long as I have, and you might find yourself surprisingly useful, too." She didn't smile as she spoke, but I could tell the two were old friends. Margaret continued, "We have been devising a way to contend with this threat to Ember Hollow. Thus far, suggestions have included protective and defensive spells, but I believe some of us have tried those and failed."

"We need to meet this witch head on." Bette again. "She's from the middle of nowhere, cut off from magic and without family. How powerful could she really be?"

I was surprised as anyone that I was next to speak, getting there before Dorothea or even Raúl. "That's a good way to ensure she'll kill more of us."

"What would you know about it?" she challenged me.

I shrugged. "Well, I witnessed Claudia Barry tearing the veil and murdering Sylvia Wright."

Another hush came over the room, at which point Dorothea thought it prudent to add, "And she's a goddamned precog. What's wrong with this town? You can't even listen to sense when it walks in the front door of your lodge." She looked at Luciano. "Now would be a moment to get me some of that wine you promised you keep in this place."

"What would you suggest, Ana?" Elena asked. "If you were there when all of this transpired, we ought to hear from you."

I felt my cheeks burn as all eyes in the lodge were suddenly on me. "Well..." I thought for a moment, ignoring Bette's scoffing face and focusing instead on my new friends and Margaret, whose expression seemed to offer me encouragement. "Claudia's method of killing began with a binding spell, and then it turned into a way to drain the witches she encountered of their life force."

Dorothea's face brightened. "Of course: bind her magic."

"If it were that simple, we would have stopped her by now," Bette said scornfully.

"Not individually," Raúl cut in, catching Dorothea's line of thinking, and mine for that matter. I wondered if all Mire witches were this way, so quick to collaborate and become of one mind. "Bind her as a collective."

"If we all work the spell together," Dorothea continued, "we can consolidate our magic to match the boost in power she's gained by killing."

I could hear witches beginning to talk amongst themselves once more, weighing whether this might indeed be the way to stop the threat to the town.

"It might not be enough," Elena warned, looking troubled, and I forgave her for her initial lack of welcome as I recognized that more than anything else, she was afraid.

"It also might kill the girl," Margaret chimed in. "Is that a risk this company is willing to take?"

Again, silence. Even in the face of murderous power, it is not in our nature to use magic to kill. Binding a witch was itself a cruel enough act that there were few witches among us who would think to attempt it under ordinary circumstances. To actually kill one of our own, by accident or design, felt like the worst thing any of us might conceive of.

"I don't see that there is much choice in the matter," Luciano finally said to the room. "If we don't attempt to bind her now, there may not be enough of us left to stop her later on."

"I can do my best to dampen her magic while the rest of you work on the binding spell," Raúl offered. "Are there any here who share that power?"

Margaret smiled at him. "It's rare to meet another witch who can soften the magic of others. You're an unusual young man."

He grinned rakishly at her, and I saw some of the witches in the crowd flush as I must have when I first encountered the full force of Raúl's striking good looks. "You have no idea, milady."

"All right," Elena moved us forward. "All in favor of binding the rogue witch?"

Much as it might be against all our instincts, the room unanimously decided that Claudia was to be bound at the first opportunity.

"Now to find her," Luciano began, but I realized that I already knew where she was.

"She's on her way to the Wright home," I said. "She's going to confront John. And he…"

They all looked at me expectantly, and I did not have the courage to articulate what horrible thing I had gleaned. Dorothea nudged me gently, and I turned, finding it easier to speak directly to her than to the room at large.

"We need to hurry," I managed. The sick feeling my powers were causing had compounded with the knowledge that we might not be able to stop what I had glimpsed would come.

"You heard her," Dorothea said to the others. "Let's go."

The scene was grim before us. The Wright home was located with the other grander houses of Ember Hollow, a part of town where great honey locusts and white pines were dispersed among the impressive properties. It wasn't often I had reason to be in that neighborhood, and now, I found what sense I'd had of the place completely banished as the strange, yellowed sky cast an eerie hue across the world. The ordinary folk of Ember Hollow knew enough not to linger or even look outside; not a door on the street was open, and curtains had been drawn in every window.

Claudia Barry was nearly unrecognizable where she stood at the base of the path leading up to Sylvia and John Wright's home. Her pallor was such that it seemed to take on the sickly color of the sky above, a greenish tint to her skin, and there were strange marks that extended up her forearms that I could not quite make out at a distance. As we drew steadily closer, I realized they were burns, scorch marks courtesy of the power she'd been draining from others of her kind, deaths that were quite literally on her hands. And all across the property in front of the Wright home, forming a veritable sea, were rats upon rats upon rats. In the short time she'd been in Ember Hollow, she had collected what I guessed was every such rodent for miles around, her influence and power stirring them into a frenzy.

Claudia did not seem to notice us; or if she did, she was preoccupied with John, who stood staunchly in the doorway of his house.

"I never asked you to come here," he was calling out to her from where he stood.

"You promised to bring me," she replied, and her voice crackled with magic, the sound distorting it so that she sounded barely human.

"You killed Sylvia!" His own words were agonized, and I could tell that he felt as much shame as anything else. Here was a man who understood his role in what had transpired between his mistress and his wife.

"She was in my way." Claudia tilted her head, as though listening to something only she could hear. "You won't stand in my way, will you, John?"

"Just go!" he shouted, anger rising in him now, and I saw him summoning his power. He took two steps forward, even as the roiling mass of rats edged towards him in a manner that could only be called hostile. And his final two words were delivered with every ounce of persuasive magic he could muster, an order that should have been irresistible to the object of his command: "*Go home!*"

But Claudia had the power of who knew how many witches running through her at that point, and the Season was amplifying her magic as much as her lover's, ten times as much as his. "I am home, John. I'm finally, finally home."

She did not need to walk up to the house to reach him. She simply raised her arms before her, and the rats gave her space as her power cracked the path all the way to the Wright front door. John lost his footing, even as he tried to summon defenses—hardly his strongest magic.

"If we're to do this, we must do it now," Margaret said urgently. "Are you ready, my charming friend?"

"After you, milady," Raúl replied, and I was glad of the cocky flirtation in his voice. It felt grounding amidst the madness.

As the two of them took one another's hands and began chanting, I saw the rats hedge in bewilderment. They felt the dampening power as much as we could see it taking effect, and Claudia turned to look at us for the first time. There was confusion on her face, but she didn't know which of us to look towards as the source of her new trouble. I realized that the power was more than just formidable; it had overwhelmed her, to an extent, and as such was confounding. Her eyes continued to shift around, seeking focus even as her magic was muted.

John saw his foe temporarily distracted, and like a fool, he threw an offensive effort towards Claudia, trying to push her back off of his property. All that did, of course, was draw her attention back to him.

"Begin the binding," Elena said, wasting not a moment as she understood that John was unwittingly about to make himself a sacrifice.

The crack in the path widened such that John's leg slid down into it, and at their witch's command, Claudia's rats no longer held back. They poured over John's body, and as he struggled, screamed, and finally succumbed to the attack of so many witch's creatures, the counterattack on Claudia began.

And this is where my own struggles took hold. There I was, amidst my peers, ready to fight with them but unable to join their efforts. It seemed that with the dawn of my new power, I was meant to witness more than to act; perhaps I was just too terrified.

Either way, every witch in my company began channeling efforts towards binding Claudia, and the effect was immediate. The scene I'd thought so cruel when Sylvia had first confronted her rival paled in comparison; in place of vines and tendrils was a flood of magic that coursed from the gathered witches out and around Claudia, thickly wrapping itself around her body like some great python chasing its own tail as it squeezed the life from its prey.

She shrieked, and the sound echoed with the caws of a thousand crows, and her birds came down from the skies and began to attack the witches below.

"Don't stop the binding!" Margaret called out, and I saw her shift her magic away from Claudia and towards the crows themselves, trying to dampen the bond they had with their witch. Raúl struggled to keep up his influence over Claudia now, having lost Margaret's support, and I saw the rogue witch suddenly push back against the bonds. The witches of Ember Hollow kept up their chanting, kept that sinuous thick snake of magic around her, and for a moment I felt a faint, traitorous stab of hope.

Then, the crows pushed past Margaret's defenses. They tore at the faces of the assembled witches, whose cries filled the air along with the calls of so many attacking birds.

"We need everyone, every bit of magic." Dorothea's voice was suddenly in my ear. "Ana, fight with us."

I could not. My head spun, sick filled my mouth, and I suddenly saw it, the world to which Claudia could escape, one of hazard and darkness where her twisted magic would live on, dangerous and deadly as ever. I saw the rats move over the bridge and through the veil, saw the sky split apart as it made room for her crows. And when she broke through the binding, I felt those same rats move in a wave through our ranks and towards the bridge, carrying their witch with them. At least half of the witches around me were dead or about to be, Luciano and Margaret among them, and even as I felt them die, my field of vision still only contained the obscurity towards which Claudia was headed, not allowing me access to the present as if my power itself knew what I could not reckon with.

A tunnel of otherworldly darkness took me, and I fell to the scorched earth beneath us, caught in a trance that was not quite enough to protect me fully from the disaster all around.

THIRTEEN

"That's it?" Gabriela said. "What happened next?"

Ana shrugged. "You know the rest. Claudia escaped into a world beyond the veil, and we barely managed to seal it behind her, given our diminished numbers."

"Dorothea made it," Maritza said softly. "What about the others?"

"Raúl survived, as well. Mire witches appeared to be made of tougher stuff than we were; at least, it seemed that way to me at the time. It was one of the reasons I found myself relocating to the other side of the bridge."

"What about the diary?" Endicott asked her. "My grandmother's note said something about you going north. Did that really happen?"

Ana nodded. "I couldn't shake what had occurred, nor could I return to any of my old haunts in Ember Hollow without experiencing intense physical reactions—panic attacks, I believe you call them now. The lodge was impossible to face, among other places, and every time I even thought of the bridge, I was terrified that the veil would open once again. So, I decided to trace Claudia's roots, hoping that doing so would give me closure."

"Did it?" Gabriela asked.

"No," Ana said. "I found an old estate that was desolate, save for a few crows keeping watch in the trees above, with a grand house that the townspeople insisted was haunted. They were reluctant to speak of Claudia. Some of the elderly residents had good things to say, reflecting more than anything a sense of duty that they felt she had demonstrated. Others seemed to avoid my gaze when I mentioned her, not with unease but with guilt, and I recognized that the house had experienced some looting and that there were no livestock where there must once have been.

"But I recovered the diary, which I knew Dorothea would appreciate adding to the Mire witch library. She was rebuilding the archive, you see—Mire had not had a librarian for some years, and the old witch library had fallen into disrepair. Dorothea was moving the site, and building up materials as best she could. I knew Claudia Barry's record of her affair with John Wright would be valuable, though it took every ounce of self-control for me not to burn the damned thing on my way back home."

"Because of all you'd seen?" Xandra asked, obviously trying to grapple with why someone would burn an important primary source text.

"Because it felt too close. Remember, I had sympathized with Claudia—seen Sylvia abuse her, take her power, devastate her. I'd sensed through my new ability what she would become and yet, how could I not feel for her, this monster who was once a misguided witch?"

They were quiet as that sentiment sunk in, and then Maritza asked, "When did you come to Mire?"

"When I returned, I couldn't go back to Ember Hollow. If anything, that feeling of panic had grown worse with my trip to the Barry estate. So, I stayed with

Dorothea for a while, and then Raúl helped me secure this place, not too far from his own home. He never said as much, but I knew it was so he could keep an eye on me, make sure I was all right in the wake of what had happened. I've lived here ever since."

"You and Raúl didn't...?" Gabriela had her eyebrows raised provocatively, such that Endicott had to stifle a snort. Her best friend did love scandal.

Ana laughed aloud. "Goodness, no—*that* would have been a disaster. No, Raúl was a dear friend to the end of his days."

"I still don't understand." Sahir was shaking his head. "Between the two magic-dampeners and the rest of you who gathered to bind her, the plan should have worked. How did Claudia escape? Was she really so powerful?"

"Power's relative," Katerina murmured, and Ana nodded in agreement.

"I believe it was hubris that kept us from binding her in the end. Had we called upon our neighbors—not just Dorothea and Raúl, who pushed their way in the door, but all of the witches of Mire—I think things might have ended differently."

A thoughtful silence hung in the room as they all digested that, and Endicott was again reminded of the letter she'd found in the folio Salomé had given them. It seemed so simple—too simple, almost—that the coming-together of the sister towns should be all it would take to defeat this great power they would be facing.

"And what is so simple about it that you can be this dismissive?" she recalled Dorothea saying to her once upon a time, when Endicott and Gabriela had a rare row and weren't speaking.

"People fight," she snapped, wanting to brush her grandmother away. "Friends fight all the time."

"Yes," Dorothea agreed. "And some friendships don't make it."

"Why do you care so much? It's just a stupid argument. Why does it matter to you?"

An unusual softness moved across her grandmother's face. "Oh, child. Don't you know that stupid arguments can end two people? Don't you know some love can't survive the inane and the foolish?"

There was so much pain in her words that Endicott knew Dorothea was talking about her own daughter. Without a thought, she'd put her arms around her grandmother and wished more than ever that her mother could be part of their embrace. There was no magic for that, though.

"We need everyone," Endicott found herself saying. "Whether or not Ana's right, we can't take that chance. If we don't stop Claudia now, both towns might not make it."

There was general murmured agreement in the room, and Xandra stood. "Let's start by heading back to the Mire lodge and enlisting the help of everyone there."

"I'll take us," Gabriela said. Endicott looked at her curiously, and she explained, "You have work to do at home, Enny—Salomé's still there, and you'll need to get her up to speed."

"The two of you will need to find a way to reach the witches in Ember Hollow," Ana added. "It is crucial you contact them as soon as you can."

"Cell phones aren't working across the bridge, but surely magic still might?" Maritza suggested, her face filled with concern.

"I wouldn't count on it," Katerina said, shaking her head. "With the bridge as it was this morning and Claudia's storm building power all day, I would imagine communication is totally cut off from Ember Hollow by now."

That settled on the group, and Endicott could see the worry in the faces of all of her friends from across the bridge as they must be thinking on their families, friends, and neighbors. Suddenly, an idea struck her.

"My hawk could get word to the Ember Hollow lodge." Then Endicott frowned. "I don't know exactly what we'd tell them, though."

"Could he fly overhead and maybe guide any Ember Hollow witches who haven't made it to their lodge?" Gabriela asked, chewing her lip doubtfully.

"Each additional trip would be a risk, especially if they're scattered around town." Judging by what they'd learned about how quickly Claudia had overwhelmed the town across the bridge the last time she'd been around, Endicott knew most witches in Ember Hollow wouldn't have likely made it to the lodge. "I don't know how long he could fly through a storm leading witches around before succumbing to exhaustion, or worse."

Sahir's eyes lit up. "We keep one creature among us that can give and receive directions, no multiple trips necessary."

They all knew that he meant bees. "To what end, Sahir?" Maritza asked her friend.

"Wherever they are at the moment, the other witches of Ember Hollow ultimately need to meet us at the bridge, right? It's too late to bring them to safety here, but they don't have to come into Mire—they just need to meet us halfway so that we can close the tear in the veil for good."

"And there are always safe paths through a storm," Katerina mused, nodding at Sahir as though she knew what he was thinking.

"Bees are small and numerous enough that they could scout out routes for our kind," he went on. "And they can tell one another where to go—they don't all have to be the ones to lead the witches directly. The network could find a way."

Gabriela was nodding now. "If Enny's hawk can get word to those who are at the lodge about the overall plan, then the bees will lead the others and we could get everyone to the bridge in time."

"That just might work," Xandra said. "But we'll have to depend largely on you at first, Endicott, so it's your call."

"My town, my call?" Endicott smirked at her affectionately.

Xandra returned the grin. "Your town, your hawk, your bees."

They all looked at her, and she shrugged. "No sense wasting any more time discussing it. Let's go."

* * *

Salomé was waiting to greet Endicott in the doorway. She waved her inside.

"You found Ana."

"Yes."

"And?"

"We're going to need everyone—both towns—if we're going to stop Claudia."

Salomé nodded. "I thought as much. But while you were gone the Mire lodge called to say they've lost all contact with Ember Hollow, magical and otherwise."

"We've thought of that, actually." Endicott filled her in as quickly as she could.

"Is your hawk ready for such a journey?" Salomé asked. "He's seemed anxious since you left."

"He'll be the one to answer that." She walked over to her hawk on his awkward perch on the chair in the solarium, and she felt his continued uneasiness, that sense that something was cosmically very wrong at the moment and he wasn't at all happy about it.

"Are you up for a ride through this storm?" she murmured, stroking his head gently with her fingertip. "I won't ask unless you're willing."

He turned to look at her at an angle, and she felt the question: how necessary was this flight in putting things right again?

"It will make a difference," she told him. "You don't have to deliver it, but I believe the right message will help us gather all the witches we need and give us an advantage in this fight." He fluttered his wings, and a smile split her face. "All right, give me a minute—I need to write the thing first, though how in the hell I'm going to manage that is still a mystery to me."

Endicott returned to Dorothea's personal library, which was where they had always kept the stationery and pens in the house. As she was sorting through one of the shelves seeking a blank sheet to write on, her hand caught the edge of another concealed envelope. Thinking that it might contain more photos from

Dorothea's past, she pulled it out to set it aside for when she had more time. Then, with surprise, she caught sight of her name scrawled on the front in her grandmother's handwriting. With shaking hands, she carefully lifted the flap and found a single folded page within.

My girl, by the time you are reading this, I'll have crossed over into another world. The house is yours and I hope you keep it; something tells me that you will.

I never wanted grandchildren, you know. Grandchildren are for the old, and I've never felt so until quite recently—and even then, the thought agitates me and I tend to brush it aside.

But I remember so clearly the day your mother first brought you to me. We hadn't spoken for years; don't ask me what our fight was about. You'll learn that such things are never as important as they seem in the moment, if you haven't learned it already. You were just a year old when we met, and she brought you into Mire under a strange and wonderful moon.

What an odd child you were! Quiet, where your mother had been rowdy; pensive, as though you did not understand this world but were determined to, no matter what it took. And you were undeniably adorable. My heart took to you before I could think twice, and so grandmother became the final and most important title I would come to bear.

Your mother left you much too soon. I know I was firm with you when you came to live with me. I had no choice; my own heart had shattered, and the strength I needed could only come forth if we were stoic together. It was on me to teach you to grow as a witch, and while I'd undertaken it once before, never had I wanted circumstance to bring such responsibility to my door again. And even with a broken heart, and even with an aging body I thought much too tired to care for an adolescent child, I found a revived purpose in life that came directly from you.

Endicott, you must understand that we are no more than what we love in this world. My magic, my library, my bees, my daughter, and you, the child of my old age, the renewed life I hadn't even known I needed—these are the legacy I leave this world. A witch cannot begin to know her own potential, but once or twice in her lifetime, if she's lucky, she'll have the chance to glimpse it.

Do not waste such moments, child. Cliché though it may sound, please heed the wisdom of this aged librarian: commit yourself to the things and the souls that you love. This letter is spelled to find you when you have need of it, especially if you've taken a wrong turn. Look around you and right yourself, my girl. You have the ability; you only need to see it.

By now, you'll be cursing me for my cryptic notes and wondering why I've never given you a straight answer. I respect you and love you far too much to have done so; I hope you know that by now. And you really can't begrudge the dead our habits, as I'd hazard to say it's far too late to change them. Instead, take a look at your own and do with them what you can.

Be well, my darling Endicott, and thrive in your power and all that it might be.

Endicott brushed at her eyes, unprepared for the surge of emotion that had taken her. All of these witches she'd recently met who'd known Dorothea, all of these stories of a life before she was Endicott's grandmother spun through her mind and left her reeling with an ache she hadn't acknowledged but that had never gone away. And she had been unhappy for a long time, now—so unhappy, as Dorothea had apparently known she would be.

But the Season had changed things, as the Season does. She felt a shift in herself, recognized that something had been stirring within her from the moment she and Gabriela had met with Xandra and Maritza in the woods. It wasn't her magic—that was still bound, kept from her. But there was something, nevertheless. It wasn't happiness, either, but the promise that if she made certain changes, if she leaned into what the magic of the Season could offer, she'd at least have a chance at...

"Potential." The word hung in the air, and it was suddenly one of many. Endicott found a sheet of paper and a pen from the shelves of her grandmother's personal library, and then she found exactly what she needed to say to the witches on the other side of the bridge.

FOURTEEN

Xandra called just as Endicott was sending her hawk out, the missive tied to his ankle. "Be safe," she told him as he pushed off her arm and into the uncertain sky. She would be able to feel if anything happened to him; every part of her hoped he would be all right.

"No one at the lodge has heard anything from Ember Hollow since before we even made it to Ana," Xandra reported over the phone. Salomé's eyes were creased with worry, and Endicott reached out to take her hand.

"What about our ranks on this side?" Endicott wanted to know. "How many are at the lodge? Do you think we'll be enough?"

"Well, that's the unexpected good news," Xandra said. "We're receiving a bit of help in that respect."

"Help?"

But before Xandra could say anything else, another voice that Endicott was not overly fond of on a good day came over the receiver. "Well, Endicott, from the last conversation I had with you and my dear cousin, how could I not stick around town for a bit? It was clear you were going to need my assistance eventually."

When she was finally able to remove her face from her palm, Endicott did her best to keep her tone even as she asked, "And what kind of help are you offering, Guillermo?"

He chuckled. "Why, long before communications shut down, I managed to contact every witch I know in the vicinity, of course."

Endicott let out a long breath. "That's actually... extremely helpful."

She could tell he was pleased as he went on. "I realize the consensus is that the collective magic of the witches in Mire and Ember Hollow will be enough to defeat this particular threat, but a little insurance never hurt anyone. Besides, the four of you have no magic at the moment, and goodness knows how many we've lost on the other side of the bridge."

"We actually have a working number," Xandra interrupted, her voice more grim than it had been.

After a moment's hesitation, Salomé said gently, "We're going to learn the body count eventually, Xandra. No sense keeping back information that could let us know where we stand, tactically speaking."

"More than forty non-witches haven't made it."

Endicott swore, but Salomé remained focused. "She's taking lifeforce from ordinary people?"

"It seems more like she's eliminating anyone she perceives as standing in her way," Xandra explained. "And several of the lives lost were people caught unprepared for the violence of the storm itself."

"What about witches?" Salomé pressed.

"We've received confirmation of twelve dead," Xandra said. "There are at least another six unaccounted for...including Maritza's aunt."

"Where is she?" Endicott asked, worry filling her chest for her friend.

"Gabriela's sitting with her and forcing a bit of tea," Guillermo replied. "You know she's good with feelings—there's no better company for such a moment."

That much was true, at least. "Do we have a sense of how many of your friends might be coming, Guillermo?"

He sighed. "Well, not everyone would have made it into Ember Hollow before it became unreachable. But I think...between Donna and her wife, and the Veremore sisters...we may have as many as seven or eight witches from out of town joining us at the bridge."

"That is good news," Salomé said, nodding fervently.

"It doesn't make up for the dead," Endicott said before she could hold the words back.

"Nothing will," the library witch replied. "But we must look to what silver linings we can. And your grandmother would not underestimate the aid of even a single witch."

And Endicott knew that was true, as well.

"So, how long are we thinking we have?" she asked Xandra. "And I guess more importantly: when do we make our move?"

"Claudia will sense the power gathered around the bridge," Xandra replied. "So time is on our side for the moment while everyone is still dispersed. How long do you think it will take your hawk to reach Ember Hollow?"

"Given the storm and the altitude he'll need...I'd guess an hour, but it might be more. These aren't conditions he's used to flying through."

"We need to give Ember Hollow a few hours to gather their forces, as well. And then the bees..."

"Right," Endicott said, letting out a breath. "It's 6:30 now, so that leaves us at..."

"Close to midnight, near the bridge," Xandra said. "Naturally."

Endicott laughed. "How did we get here?"

"I don't know, friend," Xandra replied. "But I'm glad we're in this together."

"Me too. See you around midnight?"

"Count on it."

* * *

The next thing was for Endicott to approach the hives. She had a good rapport with her bees; in so many ways, especially now that she knew about the archive, they still felt very much like Dorothea's. When she tended to them, they related to her as the beloved grandchild of their much-missed witch. As she walked in the direction of the hives, the letter Dorothea had left her rang through her mind.

"Hello," she greeted them. "I have an unusual request for you. I hope you are willing, and that you'll be safe."

The connection a witch had to her bees was both like and unlike that she had with the other creatures she kept. There was that same link that allowed her to know how they felt, to communicate freely with them, and to keep track of them wherever they might be. But there was also a nuance when it came to bees, one that kept a witch linked to the magical world around her. Bees had a magic all their own: they maintained it through language and dance, through nurture and the very fact of a hive being all of a single queen, a mother who gave life and received care from all she brought forth. They channeled energy, carrying a charge that brought pollen to rest on their tiny bodies; they created life-preserving heat through movement. And so when a witch's magic went awry, her bees were the first to know.

Claudia Barry had not kept bees. The lack of hives on her property was as bleak a reality as the lack of witches in the surrounding village. She'd been in the worst kind of isolation, and that solitude had bestowed upon her the legacy she now wreaked throughout Ember Hollow.

A witch cannot begin to know her own potential, but if she's lucky, she'll have the chance to glimpse it.

Endicott raised her hands above the hives as if casting, feeling an ache where her magic should have been. But then, the bees began to rise and rest on her outstretched fingers and wrists, reassuring her with gentle guarantees that there was hope still to be found, and what was lost for the moment could never be gone forever.

There was a feeling of being encased as more and more surrounded her, glanced across the skin of the grandchild they had been tasked with watching over, and suddenly, it was like Endicott had her magic once again. The charge of the countless workers and their beating wings seemed like power as it coursed through her, and she felt a strange certainty that the four of them—herself, Gabriela, Xandra, and Maritza—would soon be unbound once more. She shut her eyes and breathed in the scent of damp earth, of tiny bodies dusted with pollen, and then, briefly, caught a wisp of

Dorothea's perfume: faint, impossible too, but undeniable.

They all departed then, a swarm moving straight for Ember Hollow.

*   *   *

There was a knock at the door not long before Salomé and Endicott were set to leave. They opened it and found Gabriela standing there, her many hares gathered in a large group behind her.

"Why aren't you with everyone at the lodge?" Endicott asked in surprise.

Gabriela shrugged. "With Guillermo there, they had more than enough Gaud energy. Besides, we started this trip together—I wanted to be with you when we set off for the bridge again."

"You've inherited the Gaud wisdom, which has always leaned pragmatic," Salomé observed, smiling at Gabriela. "And indeed: witches who begin a thing together should finish it the same way."

It sounded like something Dorothea might have said, Endicott thought. She wanted to share the letter she'd found with Gabriela, to get her friend's take on all of the mysteries between its lines. But there was no time; they were off to face a great threat with no magic between them and only their fellow witches to rely on. Best friend bonding moments would have to wait.

As they started getting into Endicott's car, Gabriela's hares preparing to follow along outside, Endicott suddenly felt a surge in her chest and looked up to see her hawk circling. He let out a powerful screech, letting her know he'd been victorious in his trip to Ember Hollow and that he was happy to be back in his own territory. She smiled her thanks up at him, feeling ever so slightly more sure of herself as she started up the car.

The three witches rode in silence, watched by their creatures as they traveled through the night. Once they were in sight of the bridge, it became clear that they were the last to arrive. Gathered there was every witch in the town of Mire. Endicott could see some casting protective barriers along the perimeter of the town, and she understood the gravity of the battle to come. Challenged so directly, Claudia would not hesitate to turn her murderous penchant on Ember Hollow's sister, no matter how insignificant she may have thought Mire in the past.

"Are you ready?" Endicott asked Gabriela, as if they could turn around and go home.

Gabriela smiled, dug into her small bag and pulled out a handful of chocolate bars. "Always."

FIFTEEN

"It's about time you show up," Ilsa greeted them, Kace at her side.

"I don't know how useful we'll be," Gabriela said. "Our powers are still bound."

"We need everyone," Kace told her. "And along with closing that tear in the veil, we're going to figure out a way to get those powers of yours back."

"Besides, it looks like you brought reinforcements." Ilsa nodded towards Gabriela's hares, and not to be outdone, Endicott's hawk cried once more into the night.

"Didn't anyone else's creatures come along?" Endicott asked, confused.

Ilsa and Kace exchanged a glance. "Most of us told ours to stay home," Kace said gently. "But it makes sense that yours came."

"It does?" Gabriela asked nervously. "Because all of a sudden, I'm feeling like a bad hare keeper."

"It's because our powers are bound." Xandra was next to them now, along with Maritza. "Without active magic, they're our next line of defense, and they know it."

"But then, where are..." Gabriela trailed off, and Endicott knew she didn't want to make Xandra or Maritza worry about their creatures.

"My girl is okay," Maritza said with a smile. "She let me know that my bees have done their part and joined the others. She's not sure where my aunt is and I can tell she's scared, but she's putting up a strong face."

Endicott looked at Xandra, who shrugged. "At the end of the day, mine are cats."

Kace and Ilsa both looked at her in surprise, and Maritza giggled.

"I'm glad our spirits are up," Guillermo said as he approached, and Endicott found she wasn't nearly as annoyed by his presence as usual.

"Any sign of your friends?" she asked him.

"There's no way to know for certain that they made it into Ember Hollow until we see others start to arrive, but I'm sure they're on their way. Your friend Sahir is at the edge of the perimeter, waiting."

Sure enough, among the handful of witches off to one side of the bridge stood Sahir, who had his eyes fixed sharply on the Ember Hollow woods. It took Endicott a moment to realize why he would position himself so.

"He's watching for bees, isn't he?"

"He'll be the first to notice," Maritza said. "It's a shame Gabriela's sister is out of town—we could use another witch with their kind of magic."

"I'm sure we'll be fine," Endicott told her, knowing that it wasn't doubt in Sahir's abilities but anxiety over what was about to happen that had Maritza looking so worried.

Her own confidence suddenly waned as a strong gust cut through the woods. It was part of the storm Claudia had raised, marking her impending arrival at the bridge. The tear in the veil seemed to widen, and even without her magic, Endicott caught a glimpse of the cold darkness that lay there, a void waiting to expand itself out into their world.

"There," she heard Sahir saying. "Do you see them? Shine the lights."

The two witches beside Sahir, Emma and Henri, were cousins a bit older than Endicott and her friends. They had a talent for fire magic, and now both raised their hands to cast threads of flame through the darkness. There was no risk that the forest might catch fire; the two witches were in complete control of their powers, and Endicott felt a pang as she yearned to get her own magic back.

But the sight of several dozen bees leading the way along the firelit paths through the trees was enough to encourage her, as was the visible trail of witches behind them. Though the deaths they had heard of were terrible, Ember Hollow's numbers were hardly lacking. At least sixty witches approached the bridge, some of them raising a hand in greeting to those on the other side. From Guillermo's pleased expression, she knew that at least some of these were the friends he'd asked to come.

The witches who'd just arrived began to move into formation around the edge of the bridge, making sure to spread themselves out. The Mire witches had already done the same, knowing that their opponent would need to exert more effort and attention in order to tackle foes on all sides.

"What about us?" Endicott asked.

"We're supposed to take the safest position, behind that cluster of trees." Gabriela nodded in the direction she meant.

"I thought we were needed?"

"The idea is that our powers won't come unbound until Claudia loses at least some of hers," Maritza explained. "No guarantees, but hopefully we'll stay safe long enough to maybe get them back."

"That and the fact that if she sees us, she might be pissed she didn't kill us the last time we met," Gabriela added. "No sense in giving her specific targets, I guess."

Endicott frowned. "Is it wrong of me to be irritated by all this?"

"Join the club," Xandra responded.

But as more harsh, driving winds came from across the bridge, the four bound witches made their way to their designated position. Endicott was comforted by her bees and many of the others they'd recruited finding a hollow in one of the trees, trailing one another to shelter inside. She watched her hawk take to the branches above them, while Gabriela's hares found a sturdy log nearby in which to crouch. She saw Maritza's downturned face, and as she was about to offer a word of comfort about how her goose was likely safe back in Ember Hollow, a loud honk suddenly sounded in the dark. They all looked up to find the solitary creature flying across the way to Mire, her feathers ruffled but her wings strong enough to bring her to her witch.

"I can't believe you journeyed out in this!" Maritza said, embracing the goose, who nuzzled against her neck in turn.

"Have her join my hares," Gabriela suggested. "There's room, and she'll be safe with them."

Creatures secured, the four watched as the storm continued. Dark clouds expanded across the sky, blotting out stars and even covering that unmistakable

Season's moon. Those among them tasked with keeping the others as safe as they could continued casting protective barriers, echoed by Ember Hollow witches with the same talent across the way. Endicott knew that, had she her magic, Gabriela would have been working with them.

Suddenly, the ground began to tremble. Beneath those darkened clouds came a glimmering wave of crows, cawing chaos into the night on glossy wings stretched wide. Thunder rumbled above, and then the ground shook harder as a shiver of rats plunged forth, rolling booms of power following fast on their many tails. Claudia appeared as she had the night she bound them, a shadow of the woman Ana had described, a spectral length of crackling, angry magic moving with terrifying swiftness through the night.

"I'd love to know how this is going to turn out. Any chance those precog powers of yours are back?" Endicott muttered to Maritza, who shook her head, anxiety filling her eyes.

The witches at the Mire front line didn't wait. They began pushing against the wave of rats as they poured over the bridge, and Endicott saw a handful of them attempting to keep the veil from spreading further under the force of the storm.

She cursed inside herself: order within chaos. This was magic she excelled at—she always could find the calm where there were storms. And she would have been able to help if she had any power at all, but there was nothing to call on, nothing inside of her that could assist her fellow witches.

Magic sparked from the veil and it began to spread across the bridge, extending in the direction of both towns.

Out of nowhere, a hand grasped her arm. She looked up to see Xandra, eyes wide, her other arm pointed at the veil. "The veil's magic is expanding."

She nodded—anyone could see as much.

"Endicott, think: how did Claudia first get her powers back?"

"She made contact with the...but we can't go up to it, it's..." The realization hit her. "You don't think that's enough to unbind us?"

"I'm willing to chance it," Gabriela said, overhearing them. "Those protective barriers won't hold, and they need every witch available to bolster them."

"Some of us are good candidates for binding her, too," Xandra muttered, and Endicott looked at her, surprised.

"I thought you were a historian?"

"All that research and you think I haven't come across some truly fucked things our kind can do to one another, enough to learn them myself?" Xandra shook her head. "A librarian should know better."

That was the craziest thing that had been said to her in what seemed to Endicott a ridiculously long thread of crazy things. "I'm not a librar—"

"If you girls are going to try your luck," a familiar voice called to them, "you'd better try it now!"

They all turned to find Ana Flores standing behind them.

"What are you doing here?" Gabriela cried. "It's dangerous!"

Ana raised an eyebrow at her. "You barge into my home unannounced and now you want to tell me I'm too old to do battle?"

For once in their lives, Endicott found her best friend rendered speechless.

"I was a witness once," Ana said. "Once is enough. I won't stand by and watch again. Now, get yourselves to the base of that bridge and get your magic back. I'll cover you."

She began chanting a protective spell. The four of them looked at one another, and as one, reached for each other's hands.

Pushing against the winds wasn't easy, but Ana's spell helped some. Claudia wasn't attacking any of the witches present, Endicott noticed through her struggle towards the bridge. Wasn't that strange? Given her reputation and all they knew she'd done, shouldn't she be aiming to kill as many of her kind as possible?

And then she understood: the rogue witch was focused on expanding the veil as far as she could. Others had taken notice, as well. Some witches who had been prepared to aid in binding Claudia—Katerina included—now instead began lending their magic to those who were attempting to keep the veil from spreading beyond the bridge.

Endicott strained forward with all of her might; she felt every ounce of her binding, every step without magic a battle all its own. Finally, *finally*, the four of them were within range. They released one another's hands and reached their palms to the edge of the veil's power.

If it were possible for pure, unfiltered light and nurturing strength to flow into a person, that was the initial sensation of contact with the veil. All of the bonds upon Endicott released; she felt as though she'd been encased within a warm blanket of power, and the magic that was dormant within her traveled as a reassuring heat through her entire self. She smiled, feeling a little unhinged as she engaged in joy while the storm still raged around them.

And for just a moment, she understood Claudia in a way that frightened her, made her relate as Ana had told them she'd once sympathized with the murderous witch. There was an intoxicating lure in the veil's palpable power, the promise of the greatest potential of all: worlds upon worlds, all just beyond this thin boundary, all with the promise of such comforting light and strength as flowed through them now.

And then, within that lure, there was the slightest edge of discomfort. It wasn't quite pain; not yet, not as their bindings released and withered away to dust. But it was there, a razor-thin thread of that heat going just a bit too far, moving a bit too fast. Initially, she ignored it; then, seemingly out of nowhere, her hawk and Maritza's goose cried out as one. The sound wasn't so remarkable against the cries of the crows and the continuing storm; together, though, the dissonance of this call sounded by the lone birds could be heard by their witches. And Maritza and Endicott, jolted from their contact with seductive power, dangerous power, withdrew and immediately pulled their respective best friends from its reach.

Once they'd all caught their breath, Gabriela said to Endicott, "Maybe that's all Claudia really needed."

"What?"

There were tears in her best friend's eyes. "Someone who cared enough to stop her."

Xandra said firmly, "Well, we're stopping her now."

And it was as if the rogue witch had heard her words, because her gaze suddenly narrowed at them. She lifted one hand, and that sea of rats that had been roiling over the surface of the bridge suddenly began to flow directly at the four of them.

With their power back, they began to bolster the protective spell Ana had cast around them, building on its foundations, but it was taking all of their collective power to do so. The other witches around them began to struggle as Claudia fought off their defenses. She had been fixated on the veil up until now, but with witches working in every direction to stop her efforts, she finally seemed to register that she had more to contend with than what was on the bridge itself. She turned towards one group of Ember Hollow witches and started advancing on them.

Ilsa raised her hands and threw her power across the bridge, the frontal attack glancing off Claudia's arm and leaving a dark, nasty bruise. The rogue witch's lip curled, but she stayed focused on those she had aimed to attack.

"Dammit, that's my neighbor she's going for," Xandra said. "I am getting really sick of not being able to help, here."

"We need to get past these!" Gabriela cried in frustration. "How can a bunch of rodents possibly be the thing that's stopping us now?!"

But there were so many of Claudia's rats, it was all the four of them could do to try and keep them at bay.

With every inch of defense they managed to establish, a new rat would always manage to push against it, and then three more of its brethren would add to its efforts. And as the mischief began to break through their magic, countless teeth gnashing mindlessly, the witches caught fear on one another's faces.

And then Endicott saw Xandra's expression change. She laughed aloud, surprise and delight filling her eyes, and Endicott wondered whether she had in fact been in contact with the veil for just a little too long.

"Look!" Xandra pointed straight ahead.

From out of the Ember Hollow woods came nine small figures streaking wildly through the night: three black, one fiery orange, three tabby brown, one grey, and one black and white. They artfully skirted the tear in the veil as they balanced on either edge of the bridge, and then they came at the mischief and sunk their teeth and claws right into it.

"You have *nine* cats?" Endicott shrieked.

"Well, once you get past two, they just sort of pop up everywhere."

And everywhere they were. The many rats had suddenly met their match. Endicott had never known a witch's cat, but apparently, these were ferocious creatures: fast as could be and powerful, even against several rodents all at once. Her hawk suddenly seemed to sense that the battle below had shifted, and he swooped down from his perch to grab and throw a talonful of rats.

With the playing field a bit more even, the four witches were able to leave off the protection spell and finally join the battle proper. Gabriela immediately ran to Kace, Sahir, and the others who were working to keep the groups of gathered witches safe. Maritza headed over to those who, along with Ilsa and Guillermo, had started to make attacks on Claudia from across the bridge, while Xandra joined in the efforts to bind her magic.

Endicott turned to Salomé, who was deep in a spell to bring the veil together. The library witch smiled at her. "Are you ready to take up the family business, Endicott Thyne?"

Crows scattered above as lightning cracked the sky, and even with Xandra's cats in the mix, the occasional rat scampered over her foot. It was the oddest time and place to feel connected, but Endicott found that she did: to her grandmother, to Salomé, and most of all, to the task at hand.

"No time like now, right?" And she began to weave together the frayed edges of the universe where it had been split, to tame the magic that extended towards them and send it back to where it belonged.

The veil might have been a fragile thing, but it yielded to those witches intent on bringing it back together. Claudia, who had taken the life of Xandra's neighbor and two other Ember Hollow witches, suddenly turned the full force of her vitriol on Salomé and Endicott. The wave of power threw them backwards, but they didn't hit the ground. Over her shoulder, Endicott caught a glimpse of Ana and Katerina casting together to cushion the blow they'd been dealt. Salomé didn't stop working the veil for a second; and while Endicott had lost her connection to the spell, she quickly recovered it once more.

The edges of the veil drew closer and closer, and she could see the sides of the tear pull towards one another, as though the thing itself wanted to close. She sensed her magic was stronger than it had been, her ability to build order into the world more than a talent now; it was instinct, like she was one of the bees building wax into the gaps and imperfections of a hive so that all was mended and whole. And then, all of a sudden, the bridge was what it had always been once again: a link between witch towns that had feuded for far too long.

Of course, that made it only too easy for Claudia to cross into Mire, heading right for the librarians who stood directly in the way of the world she'd desired to create through chaos and destruction.

Her crows began to dive-bomb Salomé and Endicott, but they were now protected by all those witches whose attention had previously been on holding together the veil. The birds dispersed, circled back, but were unsuccessful in further efforts to attack. The rats were for their part still occupied by Xandra's cats, all of whom seemed ready to fight for days if necessary. If they weren't all in the middle of a magical battle, Endicott would swear the nine of them were having the time of their lives.

Claudia's magic was still super-charged, and the storm she'd raised continued to rage above. She began to merge her magic with those thundering clouds, throwing power up into them such that the winds that swirled about her foes were strong enough to push them off their feet, and lightning spread ominously above. As she threw more and more magic into the sky, the atmosphere became less and less stable. The bridge seemed to ripple and then tremble, and a new rift threatened to occur.

"What now?" Endicott asked Salomé, who returned the question with a troubled gaze. And if the only living library witch between the two towns didn't know what to do in this instance, Endicott surely didn't, either.

Then, soft as a breath amidst the harsh winds and rain of the storm, two of her bees came to rest on Endicott's cheek, just next to her ear. And while she didn't need to hear them to understand, she knew that what they wanted most from her in this moment was for her to listen.

Suddenly, the sound of another voice rose up. It was Maritza, back in a trance, and every witch on either side of the bridge held still to hear her words.

Witch after witch made way through the trees
Guided by thin threads of flame and by bees;
The rogue followed fast and battle ensued
And they mended the veil before she tore the world through.

The sky remained dark,
The storm wouldn't abate,
But a witch can be patient. A witch knows to wait.

And the children of Mire
and their kindred next-door
found magic enough for two sisters restored.

As one, every witch on either side of the bridge stood and began to gather their power, doing nothing to stop or harm Claudia. She did not quite seem to register Maritza's words, and Endicott wondered whether she had lost her access to language in the years she had been away. But with rage in her eyes, she continued to throw magic above, such that the clouds grew heavy with it.

Every instinct in Endicott wanted to throw a protective web above them. But along with every witch in Mire and Ember Hollow, she instead gathered her power, her hands full of heat. And she waited.

And then her bees rose from her cheek, and the rest of the colony was suddenly hovering between Endicott and the sky. Not just her colony—she recognized the presence of Gabriela's bees above, and then Kace's, and Ilsa's, and hive upon hive that had flown here to create this barrier. Horrified, the witches held their breath; Endicott knew she wasn't the only one silently pleading with her bees to move away, to get to safety. Tears streamed down Ana's face, and Endicott knew she was remembering those members of her colony that had been killed so many years before when Claudia first split the veil. But like the rest of them, the older witch waited and gathered her magic.

When the burst of power finally fell from the skies, not a thread of it came through to the witches below. Every bee was struck by the flash of lightning, and every bee fell to earth. There was a great shuddering breath that came from all the witches as each of them felt the jolt go through their bees. But in her anticipation of victory, Claudia had momentarily let down her guard. She looked in surprise at the untouched witches all around her, having been sure the storm would strike them down.

All as one, they attacked.

Endicott had never used her magic to harm another witch, but she found that she did not need an offensive spell. She used that same ability that she had tapped to weave the veil back together, to begin creating patterns and structure from entropy, and she was able to connect with the out-of-control magic emanating from the rogue witch on the bridge. There were others who were binding Claudia more directly—Xandra hadn't been kidding when she'd called herself a good candidate for such, strong and ancient spells falling from her lips as she used her newly reclaimed powers to lead the charge from the Mire side of the bridge. But for Endicott, taming the magic itself seemed the most reasonable use of her powers, and the most effective.

And, as so many witches in Ember Hollow had turned to ash from a touch of her hands, Claudia began to come apart at her very seams, becoming dust herself as the chaotic magic of the veil was ripped from her. She made no sound as it happened, but her face twisted in rage, and then in pain, and then worst of all, there was a strange look of sad regret that filled her eyes just before she became no more. The many rats suddenly stopped fighting and began to flee into the woods, Xandra's nine cats chasing them into the night with tails high. The crows and the clouds seemed to part as one, revealing the moon above.

The sight of the bees heaped on the ground was devastating, and not a witch would move for fear of stepping on a body from a beloved colony. But suddenly, under the moon's light, the ground seemed to stir, to move, and then the bees were crawling over one another and beginning to flap uncertain wings. And then they rose, and Endicott looked in astonishment at the other witches around her, not understanding this miracle they were witnessing.

Out of nowhere, Gabriela gasped, then laughed with joy. "Of course!" she cried. "My sister told me about this. Don't bees carry some kind of charge?"

Sahir nodded, smiling. "They do. Between that and the fact that they all took on the strike as one, it must have only stunned them."

Salomé looked at the gathered company and said, loudly enough for those on the other side of the bridge to hear, "We could learn much from these creatures of ours who were wise enough to come together and save every one of our lives."

"We've been talking a good deal about that, Salomé." A witch approached from the Ember Hollow side, the first to cross the bridge since Claudia had stood on it. He was in his fifties and looked fatigued from the battle, but wore the same expression of relief the rest of them had. "And it would be our honor if the witches of Mire would follow us back to the Ember Hollow lodge. We have plenty of food and what I imagine is much-needed wine, and we'd like to thank our neighbors for keeping this threat from destroying us all."

There were various expressions of surprise on everyone's faces, but Endicott noted that all of them also looked pleased. She reflected once more on a letter she had recently read, not from her grandmother but from a witch on this side of the bridge to those on the other side, telling them that they had much more in common than not. And while some things could not be reconciled—the witch who was now dust on the bridge was evidence of that—she was glad to walk across with the rest of her friends in the direction of the Ember Hollow lodge.

SIXTEEN

Although she had always known Mire's sister to have a lodge, Endicott had never visited it. Together, the witches decided that all would travel on foot, even though the way felt especially long after a night of fighting. Emma, Henri, and the others who had talent with fire magic walked with flames cupped in their palms, holding vigil for those three who had not made it through the battle.

"No Mire witches have come to our lodge before," Maritza told her as they approached. "Not by invitation, that is—your grandmother and Raúl seem to have been quite notable exceptions."

"I'm glad Tobias is the one who extended the invitation," Xandra remarked, indicating the witch who had spoken with her gaze.

"Why?" Gabriela wanted to know.

"He's always been a little..." Maritza bit her lip, trying to find the right wording. "I mean, as far as relations between Mire and Ember Hollow go, he's..."

"An absolute class snob is, I believe, the term you're looking for," Guillermo suggested, having stepped away from his friends from out of town to walk with his cousin for a bit.

Endicott looked at Xandra. "Why would he invite us, then?"

"I think it's a sign that some of the more influential people in Ember Hollow are beginning to learn that our old attitudes haven't served us for a long time." She thought about this, and added, "I'm feeling I've seen the light, so to speak."

"Can I ask you something?" Endicott asked Xandra, trailing behind the others.

Xandra hung back with her. "Of course."

Endicott hesitated, then said, "You called me a library witch."

"I did."

"What made you say that?"

An uncharacteristic smirk played on Xandra's lips. "You know, you and I have the benefit of having really kind and patient best friends."

"This is true."

"Well, sometimes that means you don't have someone in your life bluntly telling you what's really obvious that you're clearly ignoring."

Endicott opened her mouth to argue, then closed it, then opened it again, but nothing but a sigh eventually came out.

"Would it be so bad?" Xandra asked, chuckling. "Following in Dorothea's footsteps, I mean. You've already seen the archive, which is clearly badass, and then on top of that, your magic would be perfect for the job."

"It wouldn't be bad. I guess...I don't know. Maybe I'm worried I'll find something I actually like doing, and then I won't do it well. Maybe I'm worried I won't live up to her legacy." She chewed the inside of her cheek, thinking. She realized that there was a part of her that hadn't even fully accepted that there was an opening for a librarian in Mire. "Or maybe it's a little leftover resistance, like if I keep rebelling against her the way I used to, it'll mean she isn't really gone."

Xandra tilted her head, sympathy in her eyes, and Endicott wanted to accuse her of being just as kind and patient a friend as Gabriela or Maritza. Then she said, "Didn't you feel the magic in that archive? And your bees, Endicott—her bees. I'm not saying it's the same; it's not, and it won't ever be." She shrugged. "But I've never met your grandmother, and after walking around that witch library, I wouldn't ever chance to say that she's *really* gone."

They let that thought hang between them for several moments, walking in silence together in a way that could only be comfortable when witches shared each other's company.

Then Endicott said, "How on earth did you end up with nine cats, though?"

* * *

The Ember Hollow lodge was decidedly larger than Mire's, and it was more stately. As with most of the comparisons she found herself making between the two towns, Endicott found that she didn't feel slighted by taking in what was the more lavish existence of a witch in the Hollow. She loved Mire, and she had no qualms with her humble, welcoming home.

Not only did Tobias play the magnanimous host, but he made a point of circulating the room and meeting every one of the witches from across the bridge.

"So, you're Endicott," he said.

"That's me."

"I remember when you and Evelyn still lived here."

For all that she had heard her grandmother's name several times in the past days, she wasn't quite prepared to hear her mother's. "You knew us?"

"I know everyone a little," he said in the manner of a politician, and Endicott stifled a snort as Xandra passed behind him and gave a completely unsubtle eyeroll.

"Well, I'm glad you invited everyone here. I've been reading from the Mire and Ember Hollow witch archives, and it seems like having more gatherings across witch lines would do us all a lot of good."

He raised an eyebrow. "So, is the rumor I've heard true? Does Mire finally have a new librarian?"

"No." Salomé had approached, and Endicott's mouth slackened a bit at her response.

"Oh?" Tobias looked a little uncomfortable as he glanced between the two of them. "I was told—"

"The position at the Mire library is still open, pending a newly qualified candidate," Salomé went on. "But you are speaking to the new assistant librarian of the Ember Hollow library."

"Ah," Tobias replied, clearly not understanding or really caring about what was happening.

Guillermo suddenly popped up, his timing unusually helpful. "Tobias!" he said, throwing an arm over the other witch's shoulders. "Have I had a chance to introduce you to my delightful friend Donna? She's just over here..." And he led Tobias across the room, turning his head back to wink slyly at Endicott.

She laughed, then asked Salomé, "Your assistant?"

"I can't let you take up Dorothea's position without at least a little training," the other witch replied. "You've got talent, but believe it or not, the job takes a bit more than that."

"Just a bit."

They laughed together then, and rejoined their other friends. Endicott thought about the wrong turn she'd made—leaving the family business, as it was—and how it took something as grand as the Season to get her back on track. But as she looked around at friends old and new, and felt that familiar comfort in gathering with other witches, she found herself happier than she'd been in ten years or more.

And it was good to be happy, and good to be a witch.

ACKNOWLEDGEMENTS

I'm so pleased that this novella finally decided it would allow me to bring it into existence. For a while there, it fought me pretty hard, and there are several people I must thank for helping me win this particular battle.

First and always, immeasurable gratitude to my critique partners Sara Carrero, Eva Papka, and Kate Schnur. You are the three best writing partners anyone could ask for, and without your friendship, wit, and instinct, I would be lost. I also appreciate that all three of you know when to be lovingly supportive, and when to be supportively terrifying. You know that fear is a great motivator for me; please never stop being scary.

To my dear family of friends, thank you for always cheering me on. Having you in my corner means the world, and I am so grateful for your help in banishing my worries and celebrating my achievements. Thanks especially to Jonathan Alexandratos, Rachel Altvater, Tracy Bealer, Maureen Boles, Cesar Bustamante, Carmen Cabello, Catherine Carl, Kelly Centrelli, Jenny Cordella, Barbara Emanuele, Alexis Garay, Yanina Goldstein, Christina Jen, Shifa Kapadwala, Marissa Lieberman, Camille Lofters, Jessica Lynn, Robert Palmer, Megan Pindling, Rich Pisciotta, John Rice, Martha Roldan, Emily Rosewood, Jen Ross, Erik Wade, Emily Wasserman, and Omari Weekes. To my cousins Brianna Beard, Georgie Marino, and Ginalysse Ingles,

I hope this book brings back good memories of some of the loved ones we've lost.

I count myself extremely lucky to live in New York and to benefit from knowing so many creative souls who also live here. To the NYCNoWriMo community, thank you for making my Aprils, Julys, and especially my Novembers the most exciting times of the year. Extra hugs to my co-MLs Sara Carrero, Teresa Hussein, Jeremy Kerr, J King, Jessica Gregory, and Eva Papka for all the good times typing away at our keyboards and planning fun antics for the Wrimos. Thank you to the SCBWI NY-Metro community for warmly welcoming me and for renewing my excitement in writing for kids. Special thanks to my co-volunteers Susan Amesse, Lisa Anchin, and Kristi Olson for showing me the ropes and giving me a first year full of laughter and great memories.

This book is dedicated to library workers at a time when the joy of connecting patrons with the books and resources they need is slightly dampened by book challenges, actual angry mobs, and people who apparently want to throw us all in jail! I never really thought that I would find myself in such an exciting profession, but on reflection, this little book nerd has always had a taste for the radical and the revolutionary. With that said, I am so honored to serve in the field alongside some truly incredible library workers. To my work family at the Uniondale Public Library, thanks for filling my days with laughter and light. Special shout-out to the youth services warriors: James Grzybowski, Tamelee Young, Chrissy Hirsch, Lois Young, Aisha Cooper, Salamah Mullen, Lauren Rosenberg, Amanda Borgia, Lisa Paulo, and unofficially Deborah Kinirons and Jessica Gregory (because if you do enough with the collections and outreach for our departments, you're one of us!). Huge hugs to my colleagues at the libraries I've left, as well, including the Seaford Public Library, the North Bellmore Public Library, the Rockville Centre Public Library, and the Great Neck Library. And to those of you I went through the GSLIS program at Queens College with, I know that you're all doing incredible things.

I have to thank the cats in this one—after that battle scene, how could I not? Although they will never read this, Mina, Aoife, Buddy, Anya, Raven, and my dearest Inéz all played a part in my writing it, even if that part was screaming at the study door for me to stop typing and come give them food and pets already.

To my parents for their endless support and love, there is no limit to my gratitude. I'm glad you're still reading, and I hope that this book makes you think fondly of family and that it warms your heart. Con mucho cariño, siempre.

To my Danny, thank you for always believing in me and these writerly dreams of mine. I know you never doubt them, which is more than I can say, and that faith keeps me writing on even the toughest days. I love you so much.

Melissa Bobe is the author of *Electric Trees*, *Nascent Witch*, and *Sibyls*. She has published short fiction with Wyldblood Press, Urhi Publishing, Bards and Sages, and World Weaver Press. Melissa is mama to five rescue cats and one kitty spirit, and she is married to a wonderful elementary school teacher. She loves bees, ballet, cooking, and coffee. A recovering academic, she now works as a librarian.